THE WITCHING HOURS

LIAM SMITH

This is a work of fiction. Names, characters, businesses, places, events and incidents are either the products of the author's imagination or used in a fictitious manner. Any resemblance to actual persons, living or dead, or actual events is purely coincidental.

Copyright © 2015 Liam Smith

Cover photographs © 2015 Liam Smith

Liam Smith asserts the moral right to be identified as the author of this work.

All rights reserved.

First printed Anno Domini 2015

ISBN: 1512060097
ISBN-13: 987-1512060096

WITHOUT WHOM...

I thoroughly enjoyed writing this story. A huge thank you to all those who have supported my little project and seen this story through from its genesis as a blog post to its final form as a printed book. Another huge thank you to those ~~victims~~ volunteers who consented to proofread it, picking up on all my typos and reining in my over-enthusiastic employment of big words – and occasionally suggesting new ones. This is without a doubt a better book for all your help and ideas.

To be read after dark…

1764

Rain splattered the beaten track, the night restless with the clatter of the horse's hooves and the rumble of the carriage. Now and then the sky flashed with lightning, and after long seconds the growl of thunder rose all around, like the roar of seas.

The driver's face was lit by the yellow glow of the lantern swinging at his side. Water pried at the glass casing, unable to reach within and snuff out the tiny flame no matter how it tried. The coachman's eyes were narrowed, both in concentration and against the thrash of the rain. Every now and then he would cast the whip across the rump of his charges, but he doubted they could even feel it. His arse was numb from cold; so too would theirs be. Another crack of lightning, another toll of thunder. The gap between light and sound narrowed: the storm was getting closer.

Daniel was somewhat drier in the body of the coach, though his boots still dripped with the black graveyard mud that had sucked at them half an hour before. He'd stared out of the window for a while as they'd left the village, but had given up once they'd hit open country. Now the only sights available were lit by forks of lightning and veiled behind rivulets of rain, and they held no comfort for him. Trees and fields. The odd scarecrow spun wildly in the racing wind. He looked down at his gloves, the leather worn pale from the rough handle of the spade. The carriage jolted over ruts in the road and he could hear the splash of the wheels trawling through puddles beneath the tattoo of the horses' hooves. Upon crossing a particularly large dip or peak, the coach would jar angrily, and the coffin before Daniel would clunk on the wooden floor.

The driver was first to notice the sound. Though his mind was otherwise distracted, he was attuned to the symphony of the horses, the percussive rhythm of their gallop, the snorts of their labour. An echo rode on the wind, an echo of the horses' gait. Another travelled the road this night. Gripping the reins, the coachman shifted on his seat to check the track behind him. He could see nothing, but thought he caught a stray whinny on the wind. He twisted to look around the other side of the carriage but the rain drove into his face. The sound of strange hooves was growing louder.

Daniel heard the sound too and muttered a prayer into the dark night.

A traveller. Just an innocent, riding home to his bed.

He thought of his cargo and knew it would not be so.

The driver tossed the reins and snapped the whip across the straining hindquarters of the horses. Daniel watched him through the slit window at the front of the coach. He felt in the pockets of his coat and withdrew a pistol and a bag of powder. He heard a bray from the road behind as he loaded the weapon.

Rain lashed the driver's face as he risked another look back. As he did so the lightning flashed and for a moment the world was as bright as a summer's day. The image froze like a painting in his mind: the cloak of cloud spread overhead, the bumpy road stretching back as far as the eye could see. The black-clad figure, bent low on its steed, in hot pursuit of the coach. As if in resignation, the driver gave the reins one last flick.

Daniel watched through the thin window as the figure galloped past the coach. He saw the rider pull something from his cloak and a moment later there was a bang and flash that had nothing to do with the storm. He felt the jerk of the carriage as the horses started, and peered through the front window. His driver was unharmed. He turned back to the door window to see the black rider aiming up at the coachman. A flick of the gun-hand. A signal to stop. Daniel clutched his own pistol in a clammy hand.

The carriage rumbled to a halt by the side of the track. The moonlight did little to illuminate the scene; all Daniel could see was the fence separating field from road. Crops trembled in their ranks. The stranger kept his gun trained on the driver and swung down from his horse. He indicated for the driver to do the same. The lower half of his face was masked by a cloth, and he reached for a tricorn hat fixed to the saddle of his mount, settling it on his head to keep the rain out of his eyes.

'How many inside?' he called out.

'Just the one sir. We carry no money, no goods that would be of interest to you.'

The assailant cocked his head.

'You know nothing of my interests.' He waved his gun towards the door. 'Open up.'

Daniel watched the exchange and tucked his own pistol under his black cloak. He saw his driver approach the door and, after a concerned glance through the window, open it. The highwayman stepped forward, gun pointing into the carriage.

'Out you come. Stand and deliver.'

Daniel wrapped his cloak around him and climbed down the wooden steps. He slipped a little, but could not reach out to steady himself with his hand already round the butt of the pistol. He regained his balance and squelched down into a deep puddle. Water flooded his feet and rain soaked his face.

'We have nothing to give you. Had we anything it would be yours. But we carry nothing of value.' He spoke bitterly, and the rain flecked from his lips.

'I think I'll decide that for myself,' the highwayman responded. He reached for the carriage lantern and unhooked it. His horse snorted and then started to piss. It steamed in the cold. The thief stepped to the back of the coach and grunted at the empty rails.

'No luggage,' he said out loud.

'As I said,' replied Daniel. He caught the eyes of his driver and nodded. Flicked his own eyes down at his cloak, trying to signal his plan. The highwayman turned.

'No luggage on display that is.'

He placed a foot on the step and then paused. He looked at the two men. The driver, his face weather beaten, his clothes soaked through. The passenger, shivering in fresh exposure to the elements, huddling into himself. The highwayman pointed the gun at the driver.

'You. Go first. What are you carrying?

The driver stepped up and into the coach. He stepped over the coffin. The thief kept his gun trained before him, and pointed the lantern into the darkness of the carriage. An eyebrow raised when he saw the casket. The other followed when he heard a click behind his head.

'Another step sir, and it will be your last,' said Daniel. The gun in his hand trembled a little from cold, but at this range it wouldn't matter. 'Hands in the air. Keep hold of the torch. Drop the gun.'

The highwayman bit his lip. The rain kept falling. Daniel felt the water squelch in his boots.

'I said hands in the air.'

The highwayman raised his hands.

'And drop the gun!'

At this the thief smiled.

'I'm afraid not. What kind of outlaw would I be without a weapon?'

'I will shoot you.'

'Then pull the trigger.'

A lightning flash, and thunder a second later. Daniel looked at the coffin inside the coach. And fired.

A damp click. He pulled the trigger again. Nothing.

The thief turned and aimed his own weapon at Daniel.

'You might have remembered to cover your gun from the rain.' He waved his own gun, where the locking mechanism was covered by a leather shield. 'Now. Your money or your life.'

'We have nothing for you.' Daniel spat the words out in defeat.

'As you wish.' The gun flared and Daniel felt a pain like a hard punch in his gut. He felt his useless pistol drop from his hand, and stumbled back a step. The thief turned his attention back to the driver.

'You. Open it up.' He gestured to the coffin. The coachman obeyed without a word, hauling at the lid of the coffin till it slid upwards, the nails releasing their hold. The thief grunted. He'd expected his victims to have hidden their valuables within, but it looked to contain a genuine cadaver.

'All the way now. I want to see if your friend died for nothing.'

The driver cracked the lid off and dropped it to the floor of the carriage. Thunder and lightning struck simultaneously. The highwayman brought the torch in close.

The body was that of a woman. She looked freshly dead. The skin was very white and her clothes hadn't mouldered.

'Who is she?' asked the thief.

'She was his wife,' muttered the driver. He couldn't see Daniel's body past the glow of the lantern.

'And now she will see him in the afterlife.' The murderer prodded at her cheek with the barrel of his pistol, and stroked it down to her breasts, still firm. Very fresh indeed. 'And what is this...'

The brass tip of the gun clinked softly against the chain of the pendant hanging round the woman's neck. He squinted to see it in more detail. It seemed to be a jewel surrounded by elaborate metalwork. He looked closer: a ruby treasure guarded by exquisitely carved strands of silver.

The highwayman stripped a glove from one hand with his teeth and spat it onto the floor of the carriage.

'Don't try anything,' he warned. The gun remained in his right hand. Without taking his eyes from the driver, he felt for a clasp on the pendant chain, fingers lingering for just a moment too long on the dead woman's breast swell, then on her ear lobe. He unclipped the fastener and lifted the necklace before his eyes. The chain was striking, alternately silver and red. The jewel fascinated him, and it was all he could do to stop from staring at it. Wrenching his eyes away, he slipped it into a pocket inside his coat.

'My thanks.' The highwayman lowered himself back down the steps. He hung the lantern back at the front of the carriage. The driver had yet to emerge. He removed his hat and tied it back to the saddle of his mount, and re-holstered his weapon. He hauled himself onto his horse, and trotted to the coach door. The driver knelt before the coffin. His gaze shifted from the casket to dark ground outside, where the body of Daniel surely lay.

'I'm sorry for your friend,' said the highwayman. He wasn't.

'I'm sorry for you,' said the driver.

The highwayman looked at him quizzically. Then spurred his horse and wheeled around, riding back down the road, leaving his victims behind him.

Above, lightning flashed. After several seconds, the thunder roared its answer.

2014

'What a find!'

Richard clunked the boot of the Fiesta shut, careful not to bump the antique hatstand as he did so. He plonked himself down into the driver's seat.

'Comfy?' He slotted the key and turned and the stereo began to play. Lucy glared at him from behind the head of the hatstand.

'It would be comfier without this in my face,' she said. Then smiled: 'Worth it though!'

'We could do with a bigger car if we're going to keep this up.' Richard reversed, braking hard as another car whizzed past behind, looking for a space. 'A five door, maybe.'

'We won't afford one at this rate,' Lucy said. 'But I'd prefer to have a house full of nice things and a small car than a dumpy flat and a BMW.'

'Speaking of nice things, where are we off to next?'

'Aah... Take a left here. I know we want to go in that rough direction.' Lucy pulled her notebook from her handbag and flipped to a bookmarked page. 'Innswich is next on my list. Here's the postcode...'

'I'd be happy if we went home with what we have now. We've certainly had a bit of luck today.'

'Always room for more! Maybe not in this car...'

Richard spotted the sign for the A-road as Lucy tapped the postcode into the sat nav. Minutes later they were motoring on towards the next picturesque village in the trail laid down in Lucy's notebook.

It was a bright autumn afternoon – the kind where summer's warmth still lingers and the trees have only just begun to rust. Richard had his shades on and an arm propped up on the car door. Lucy gazed out of the window. The world outside was beautiful: fields on all sides, clumps of trees beyond. The road wound easily through it all, with barely any other traffic to negotiate. When Richard stopped at a junction they both admired the old-fashioned wooden signpost that pointed them in the direction of Innswich.

'Look at that,' pointed Lucy. Richard flicked his eyes away from the road. There was an old church further on ahead.

'Maybe that's Innswich,' he replied.

'It looks like it's all on its own.' Lucy looked at her watch. 'It's not even three yet. Let's stop for a look, I brought my camera.'

'Sure, why not.' He slowed till a turning presented itself, and followed a narrow lane up to the church. He parked at the side of the road, against the old stone wall surrounding the churchyard. Lucy disentangled herself from the hatstand and together they unlatched the stiff iron gate, weaving through the headstones and up to the church.

Richard liked churches, although he hadn't realised it until Lucy had taught him about history. Churches were like historical barometers, apparently. Religion was a huge part of life in the old days and churches exhibited both the love of patrons and the wrath of enemies. Richard supposed it was a lot easier to like something once you had been taught a bit about it.

'Move Richard,' called Lucy. She was crouched down further back along the path with a camera against her face and one hand gesturing him to move. He did. She trotted up after a few snaps.

'It's strange to see a church in the middle of nowhere like this,' she said.

'Well, God is everywhere.'

'Even so.' Lucy was oblivious to Richard's smirk. 'People usually build them where they live. And from the photos it looks like the spire is a bit crooked.'

'How strange. You want to take a look inside?'

'Absolutely. Come on!'

Lucy led the way up to main door but was stopped at the entrance to the porch by a black iron grating. She gave it an experimental rattle. Richard shrugged a jacket on. It was a bit chillier in the shade.

'I don't think it can open.' Lucy poked the big weathered padlock. 'This is weird as well. Usually if a church is all closed up it will have been done by the council. This lock looks too old for that. It looks nineteenth century, or older.'

Richard counted in his head.

'That's the eighteen-hundreds.'

'Mmm. Very odd.'

'Maybe everyone moved away. No one left to use it.'

'Maybe...' Lucy lined up a photo of the gate, a dead-on shot that emphasised the asymmetry caused by the bloated padlock. 'We can still look round the outside though.'

They wandered. The grass was long and there were weeds in it. *But no rubbish*, Richard noticed. *That's nice.*

'Crooked, see.' Lucy's camera clicked again. Richard could see it now: the spire was bent. Not sunk on one side, but cricked in the middle. It reminded him of a finger, sticking up into the sky, slightly bent at the knuckle.

'That's the Devil's door,' he said, pointing at the miniature wooden door on the other side of the church. Lucy smiled at him.

'You remembered! I take it we can't get in through there...' She bounded up to the door and tugged at the iron ring. 'Nah...'

Richard zipped up the jacket. It had definitely turned cold in the past few minutes.

'Try it again? Could've sworn it moved.'

Lucy hauled at the old ring for a few seconds. Just as she let go, there was a clunk and creak from inside the doorway.

She and Richard looked at each other.

There was another creak. Like a board creaks up in the attic at night, for no reason. Cold wind rustled the leaves and long grass.

Richard nodded at her. She turned the ring and pulled again. Nothing now.

'Letdown,' she murmured. Richard nodded.

* * *

Innswich was a traditional English village. As they pulled into the high street they were greeted by the town coat-of-arms atop a tall wooden pole. Lucy was pleased to see a prevalence of independent shops: a newsagent, hair salon, a few coffee shops – there was even a self-proclaimed *Brocanteur*, a quaint little boutique nestled in the run of high-street stores. Lucy made a note of that one. This wouldn't be a proper antique-hunt if they didn't investigate such an idiosyncratic little place.

Richard found a little car park behind the main street (free for two hours) and the couple held hands as they took a stroll down to their intended destination – Innswich Emporium.

Antique hunts were a tradition in Richard and Lucy's life. Perhaps twice a year, sometimes coinciding with a birthday, the two of them would decide on a county in England, and investigate the antique shops both on the way there and in the area. They'd make a snap decision late on Saturday afternoon and find somewhere to stay – a bed and breakfast, a hotel, a pub. Part adventure, part shopping trip. Part dirty weekend. On Sunday they would return to their house and add to it another characterful furnishing.

Lucy had picked out a few likely-looking purveyors of the vintage and antique, and noted down their addresses prior to the trip. Innswich was the last of their must-visit villages – their third today, though they'd stopped at a stone circle for a look around too. There were a few maybes that could make the cut on the return trip tomorrow.

The perusal of an antiques shop would always begin with the inspection of the windows. Innswich Emporium's windows had roll-down gratings that would protect it after closing time. This didn't necessarily mean a shop would have more expensive stock, Lucy had discovered. But in antiques shops, expensive items weren't always the valuable items.

Their window-shopping didn't reveal too many surprises: dark wood furniture, an artistically arranged tea set. A bookcase visible in the relative gloom of the shop floor. Richard gave Lucy the nod, and in they went.

By the time they had finished it was half four. Richard had hummed and ha'ed over a moose head but Lucy had put her foot down.

'It's got a lecherous grin,' she claimed. 'We'll get you one of those plush ones. Cute and with a sense of humour.'

The sun was still up though, and the sky clear. A day when winter seemed a little further away than it really was. Lucy dragged Richard down the street, eager to have a quick look around Innswich's *Brocanteur* before closing time. It was a curious little shop, perched on the end of a terrace of other stores (a butcher, model shop and barber) as if trying to be part of the crowd. Its name was written in loopy italic script above the door and windows. A sign hung behind the glass door: *Come In, We're Open!* After a quick peek in the windows —one full of books and brass and watches, the other displaying furniture – Lucy twisted the old handle and stepped into the shop.

The sense of quiet was tangible. Even when there

are other customers in these kinds of shops, the presence of old things usually hushes voices and softens steps. There was no one else inside that Lucy could see. The shop was quite small, with shelves against all the walls, and glass exhibition cabinets forming an island in the centre. She began to work her way round the displays. Richard's eyes had settled on a table of old LPs in one corner and he started to thumb through them.

Lucy passed old globes and telescopes, teapots and trays, boxes and lamps. She tickled the thinning fur of a taxidermy cat and tapped her fingers experimentally on a tribal-looking drum. She brushed the spines of old leathery books and thought better of blowing into a rusting harmonica. Her tour of the shop brought her round to the counter, and to the glass display cabinets. Then something caught her eye.

The cabinets were stacked with so much clutter – some of it valuable, she supposed. Lockets propped open, keys on chains, elaborate teaspoons. Rings, bracelets, earrings, pearls. Necklaces. Pendants.

She touched the glass with her fingertips. The pendant was resting on a green velvet-effect cushion. At its heart was a red stone, cut to an almost-perfect circle. The bottom arc was pointed slightly, pulling it into a wide teardrop shape. It was deep, deep red – like piano music, Lucy thought to herself illogically. Like the sound the low keys on a piano make. Around the stone were woven strands of silver, knotting together in a Celtic fashion. The chain seemed to grow out of the metallic nest, its links alternately red and silver.

Lucy realised she'd crept closer to the cabinet when her breath began to mist the glass. She pulled away and glanced around the shop. Richard had abandoned the records and was moseying around the displays just as she had. She gave a start when she saw the ghost face of a stranger reflected in the glass in front of her. Whipping round, she saw a man behind the counter. She assumed he was the *brocanteur* himself; a middle aged and slightly dusty man, all messy hair and salt-and-pepper stubble beard. She noticed an open door behind him – she hadn't even registered it before. He watched her, patiently. She raised a hand a little in greeting.

'Hi,' she said.

He smiled back at her.

'Good afternoon, young lady. Have you come far today?' His speech was perhaps a beat too slow, but it didn't make him sound unintelligent. It made him seem patient, as if time was not a concern.

Lucy glanced at Richard, who was fiddling with something on a shelf.

'Just a couple of hours down the road. We just thought we'd pop in for look around...'

The man nodded kindly.

'And has anything piqued your interest?'

Lucy smiled instinctively, the way someone will upon hearing the name of the secret object of their infatuations.

'We're only browsing. Only... Well, I was admiring something here, in the cabinet. A necklace. May I ask you about it?'

The man smiled and stepped out from behind the counter, pulling a small bunch of keys from his pocket. He eased one into the cabinet lock and slid back the glass panel. Carefully, he removed the green cushion and held it up to Lucy. She felt a hand automatically reach for it, then stopped herself. He nodded.

'Take a closer look. I trust you.'

She lifted the pendant from its perch with one hand and caught the chain with the other. She examined the necklace, fascinated. The central stone was amazing; she looked into the heart of it as if it were a deep red lake. The pattern around it would have made a beautiful design in its own right, but here seemed to curl around the stone, protecting it.

'The knotwork is sterling silver,' advised the *brocanteur*. 'And the chain alternates sterling and enamel links. I believe it was made in Elizabethan times.'

'Where did it come from?' asked Lucy. The stone caught the light of the bulb overhead and flashed as she turned it.

'It was sold to me by an old gentleman from a neighbouring village; I found it in a box of miscellanea. A death in the family, I supposed.'

'And what is the stone? Ruby?'

The man smiled.

'Actually, I think it's just glass. Flawless, I know. It was probably made completely circular, but has slowly settled over time into the teardrop shape you see now. Glass is, physically speaking, a liquid you know.'

Lucy nodded.

'It's beautiful.'

'What's beautiful?' Richard edged around the cabinets and peeked over Lucy's shoulder.

'Richard. I was just admiring this necklace. Isn't it gorgeous?'

Richard nodded, appreciating more the keenness

in Lucy's face than the pendant itself.

'How much is it?' he asked the shopkeeper. The man named his price.

'Done.' Richard slipped out his wallet. 'I like treating my wife. And whilst you're there, I spotted a fantastic carved box on the shelf over here...'

* * *

It was dusky by the time they arrived back at the car. Richard started the engine and flicked his lights on.

'So which way do we go?'

Lucy had asked the *brocanteur* if there were any hotels nearby, somewhere they could stay for the night after grabbing a bit of dinner. Innswich doesn't have any, he told them, but Milbury offers some accommodation. Lucy was sure she'd seen the way to Milbury earlier, on the old sign they'd admired at the junction in the road.

'Back the way we came, a little. Past the church.'

Richard pulled away, his beams illuminating just a little of the road ahead. They passed the collections of little independent shops and the creaking Innswich signpost, and slipped away onto the winding country roads. The sky ahead was clear, but Lucy could see dark clouds starting to bubble over the village of Innswich behind them. The fields rustled on either side of the road and, when the car passed clumps of trees, Lucy found herself staring into the dark nests of shadows that were made. Richard was listening to something quiet on the stereo, something with piano and soft guitar, and it sounded warm. She supposed the evening outside was cool now, and quiet. She saw a black mass out over the fields and deduced it was the church they'd stopped at that afternoon. Sure enough, Richard slowed the car as they approached the junction from earlier. He and Lucy peered out at the old signpost.

'We just came from Innswich...' he muttered.

'So onwards to Milbury!' Lucy finished. Richard shifted back up a gear and the car continued onwards, a roaming golden light in the grey of night.

* * *

Milbury was smaller than Innswich. Richard took his foot off the accelerator and turned the stereo down.

'He definitely said there would be a place to stay here?'

They drove slowly down a street of houses, many of them old. A few cul-de-sacs branched away from the road. A light rain started to silently speckle the windscreen.

'Definitely. A "public house" – his words.'

Richard tapped his fingers a little on the steering wheel. He'd been driving all day and, while he didn't dislike it, was ready for a pint and a hot meal. A small wooden signpost pointed off down another turning. Richard squinted.

'High Street,' murmured Lucy. 'Try down there.'

They turned, passing a few more houses and an old red telephone box. It was night-time proper now, and their headlights provided the only useful light. Most houses glowed like reluctant lanterns, their curtains drawn to hold the light inside. A shallow stream ran parallel to the road, and small bridges led across it to the houses on the other side. Twice they caught sight of figures walking along that opposite bank, but Richard refused to stop and ask for directions. No matter – after passing a farmhouse on the left a welcome sight presented itself. A thatched-roof pub, white washed walls and black timber beams, its windows lit warm and yellow. Richard eased the car over a narrow bridge and headed behind the pub to a small car park.

They gathered their rucksacks and coats from the back seat before clambering out of the car. The rain wasn't too heavy but they still jogged to the pub's porch, grateful for the opportunity to stretch their legs. Beneath the porch roof, they straightened their attire, the better to make a good impression. The door was a thick, studded oak affair, and Richard found himself unable to resist a soft tap of the knocker – a weighty piece of iron carved into an equilateral Celtic cross. He pushed the door open with a low creak and the couple entered the pub.

The desk in front of them was empty. Richard could see a bar curving round to the right and hear chat and laughter. There must be a fire too; it was warm inside and the air smelled of wood smoke. On their left was what looked like a breakfast room or afternoon tea parlour. They both shuffled further in as the door behind them creaked open and an old bearded man scowled his way past them, heading towards the bar. Richard caught Lucy's eye.

'Locals seem friendly,' he smirked.

A young man appeared from around the corner.

'Evening,' he smiled. 'Anything I can help you with..?'

Richard nodded.

'Just wondered if you have any rooms free for tonight.'

The man cocked his head.

'I'll just have to check with the manager. Please excuse me...'

He took his leave through a door behind the desk. Richard saw the foot of a staircase just before the door clunked shut.

'Shall we grab a pint?' He raised his eyebrows suggestively as chitchat swelled behind him in the bar area.

'Let's wait a moment. We should make sure we'll be sticking around first.'

There was a slow clump from behind the door and it was pushed open with a little effort from an older man. He nodded to the young couple.

'Madam. Sir.' He slipped behind the desk and beckoned them forward. They approached. Lucy tugged at Richard's sleeve and pointed at the business cards and information pages on the desk. All were scribed with a logo and the pub name:

The Hanged Cat.

Richard made a moue. A little gothic perhaps, but here they were in deep English countryside. A little blackened quirk was to be expected, and it wasn't like there were pentagrams daubed onto the walls.

'You require a room for the night?' the old man enquired. His voice and movements were slow, but his fingers tapped with impatience.

'Please. Just the one.'

'One room, or one night?' the man replied. There was something of a sneer about his mouth, Richard thought.

'Both, I suppose...'

The man shuffled some papers.

'We have three rooms available, but you shall be our only guests tonight. Payment is upfront.'

'Is card ok?' Richard placed his wallet on the counter. The old man looked puzzled for a moment.

'Ah, you mean to pay by credit card,' he said. Richard brandished his Visa.

'Debit actually. Couldn't get a decent credit rating.'

The old man leered at the card but took it anyway, making a show of seeking out a dated card reader, leaving Richard to thumb through the prompted screens before inputting his PIN. Outside, the light rain intensified, building to a steady batter on the glass. The machine took its time computing, and Richard caught Lucy's eye. She gave him a quiet smile. Richard handed the machine back.

'And will you be dining with us tonight?'

Richard turned to look at the window. Rain lashed the remote village and there came a sudden flash of lightning. He turned back to the publican, and waited for the thunder roll before replying.

'Oh, I should think so.'

* * *

Lucy brushed her hair in front of the mirror. Through the open door she could see Richard lying back on the bed, already in jeans and shirt. She supposed it was true: men could get ready faster. But then, he'd been first in the shower.

She wondered when the moment had come in

their relationship when they'd stopped closing the bathroom door. Richard had happily peed, showered and shaved without needing any privacy, and now she was comfortable to stand, still naked from her shower, before that same open door. It was nice to feel trusted and trusting, secure with her husband in that way. But Lucy wondered whether it was a shame: a shame that their nakedness was now taken for granted. That it was no longer the mark of sensuality – and, yes, sexuality – that it had once been.

'What do you fancy for dinner Luce?' called through Richard. He'd rolled onto his stomach and was fiddling with his watch.

'Not sure, I'll see what's on the menu. I am in a pub grub mood.'

'Steak.'

'Maybe. Steak can be risky if it isn't excellent, because I can do a pretty good steak myself.'

'True.'

She finished brushing her hair (still a little damp – the provided hairdryer hadn't been up to much) and wandered back into the bedroom.

'Oh Richard!' She closed the curtains before the Milbury locals saw a little too much. 'Just because it's dark out there doesn't mean that strangers can't see in!'

'Ah, no one's watching.' Richard sat up and rested a hand on her side. 'You look hot.'

'Thank you Richard...' Lucy prodded through her pile of clothes till she found her knickers, and pulled them on, snapping the band round her hips. Richard watched with a smile. She slipped her bra on and took a moment finding the clasp. She stuck out her tongue at her husband, whose smile had broadened, appreciatively. She picked up a black dress and stepped into it, covering her body once more.

'Would you zip me up?' She turned her back to Richard and held her hair up clear of the fastener's teeth. A moment later she felt the soft touch of one hand on the zip, the other more firmly on her waist. Just before he finished, she felt the little brush of his lips against the top of her back, and she smiled.

'And whilst I'm here...'

Richard leaned across to the other side of the bed, to Lucy's bedside table. He took the green felted box from it, opening it with a muted click, and withdrew the pendant from inside. A bar of light slid across the incarnadine shard as he tilted it in his hand. Outside, the rain splattered against the window.

Lucy smiled in expectation, then in pleasure as she felt his hand circle her neck, draping the chain about her. The silver and the stone were cold, but warmed quickly against her skin, below the hollow of her throat. She felt the clasp come together round the back of her neck. Richard turned her around.

'It looks lovely on you.'
'Thank you Richard.'
She tiptoed and kissed him on the lips.
'And thank you for buying it for me.'
'My pleasure. Dinner's on you.'

* * *

Richard got his steak, and a pint of something dark. Lucy had taken a chance on the wine menu and compounded her chosen tipple with a particularly ungraceful, if tasty, beef burger.

The restaurant area was down past the bar. Part of it was a glazed conservatory, but they had opted to sit near the fireplace in the pub proper – the rain was thrashing down heavily, striking the glass conservatory like God's fingers might tap on a snow globe. There were a few other diners: a couple at a table on the opposite wall, and a group of five at a table for eight. A few drinkers had braved the damp clatter of the conservatory. *At least it's dry,* thought Lucy. She pitied the smokers.

Richard downed knife and fork to an empty plate and swigged at his pint.

'Tasty that,' he observed.

'Your beer?'

'The steak. Cut like butter and just melted on the tongue. The beer's good too though.'

'The Hanged Cat?'

'Mmm. There must be a brewery nearby I guess, and the ale got named in honour of the pub. You want to try some?'

Lucy finished her last fat chip and nodded. She took a sip.

'It's nice.'

'Not just nice. Rich, textured, deep. Smooth.'

'I'm glad you like it.'

Lucy set the glass back down on his side of the table and propped her face in her hands.

'I love you Richard,' she said.

'Yeah?'

'Mmm. Remember when you proposed to me?'

It had been on a fledgling antiques hunt that

Richard had popped the question. The two of them had driven north on their own grand tour to view castles and ruins, and spend the night in a Victorian guest house. A nearby town had yielded an interesting little shop, a warren-like place full of low ceilings and tottering shelves. Richard, his attentions perhaps just a little more prone to wander, had strolled through the winding aisles ahead of his girlfriend...

*

Lucy rounded a tall dresser unit and found her boyfriend scrutinising something in a tall glass case.

'What've you found?' she squeezed his arm.

'Ah, nothing,' he replied, and he pulled her onwards. 'Just killing time whilst you were browsing.'

They spent another half hour in the shop investigating furniture, trunks and smaller bric-a-brac. Richard prodded through a selection of hats, but he seemed a little quiet. Lucy put it down to one of his moods; they could come on quick sometimes. He wouldn't be grumpy exactly, just not very talkative. Thoughtful.

They re-emerged into sunlight with an elegant table lamp and wandered back down the high street to the car park. Richard unlocked the car then paused. He slipped out his wallet and peeked inside.

'Shit. I think I left my card at the shop.'

'Oh no. Let's go back. I'm sure the lady will have hung onto it for you.'

Richard nodded.

'Tell you what. I'll just go back. My legs are longer than yours.'

'You sure?'

Lucy's eyes had already dropped to the chick-lit paperback lying on the passenger seat.

'Yeah. It'll give you ten minutes of peace to read, won't it?'

'Ok. Good luck, see you soon.'

Richard strolled off. Lucy locked the car from the inside and nestled back into the seat, absorbing herself in the pastel-pink novel. After five minutes she cracked a window open. It was a warm day.

Richard had been fifteen minutes. Lucy started at the sudden *clunk* of the central locking and closed her book in time to greet her boyfriend as he swung himself down into the driver's seat.

'You look pleased with yourself,' she commented.

'Do I?' Deadpan.

'Did you get it sorted?'

Richard's eyes smiled.

'Yeah, it's all good. All sorted.' He revved and reversed. 'Shall we go find this hotel?'

They arrived at the guest house after stopping off for a pub lunch. It was a gorgeous building of red and yellow brick, full of pointy roofs, dormer windows and even a quixotic tower. More of a mansion than a house. After checking in they threw their bags in their room, a snug space with dark wood beams, ornate wallpaper and idiosyncratic furnishings – not least a medieval revival-styled headboard. Then they went out to explore.

Richard was still quiet, but Lucy linked an arm

through his as they wandered through the hotel's expansive grounds. They wandered through trees and over wooden bridges, and Lucy took the opportunity to take some photos of the light rays slicing through leaves and branches, of the whispering stream that flowed past the house and of Richard, smiling, leaning against a fence post.

> They started to head back to the house.
>
> 'Love you Lucy,' said Richard.
>
> She hugged him as they walked.
>
> 'You too,' she beamed at him.
>
> 'Could I take your photo with the hotel in the background?' asked Richard.
>
> 'Sure,' she replied. She stood, happy, smiling. Richard snapped a photo.
>
> 'Can't quite get the tower in,' he called.
>
> She rolled her eyes, good-naturedly. He knelt, one knee settled in the grass, and snapped again, a few times.
>
> 'Come a bit closer,' he said. She did.
>
> 'A little further.'
>
> He took one more photo and beckoned her closer. He put the camera down behind him. He looked tense.
>
> 'Lucy,' he started. She looked down at him, quizzical, warm. 'I didn't know when to do this, but... I just couldn't wait.' He reached inside his jacket pocket, and retrieved a small box. Lucy's heart stopped and she forgot everything else in the world.
>
> 'Lucy,' said Richard, opening the box and looking up into the heart of her, 'will you marry me?'

*

'Here's to us,' toasted Richard. He held up his pint and Lucy clicked her glass against it. 'I think we've done pretty well.'

'Indeed, my husband, indeed.' Lucy sipped the last of her wine. Her engagement ring, a band of gold crowned with a coral-red stone, nestled on her finger. She stroked it absent-mindedly.

'What do you say to having one more at the bar and then heading up to bed?'

'It's only nine o'clock,' Lucy protested.

'Exactly,' Richard winked.

They headed to the bar. The young man from earlier was tending, but for the minute he was unoccupied. A couple of middle-aged men sat on barstools, engaged in stop-start yet comfortable conversation. The couple who'd been eating dinner had gone but the larger party remained, providing enough merriment for the whole establishment. The bearded man who had huffed past them earlier sat in a corner beneath a window, ignoring the rain whipping hard against the pane.

Richard ordered another Hanged Cat, while Lucy switched to a gin and tonic.

'Are we ok to charge this to the room?' Richard checked. It was.

Lucy settled herself on a stool but Richard preferred to stand.

'Have you got anywhere marked for tomorrow?' he asked.

She shook her head.

'If we go back a different way than we came, we're bound to pass somewhere interesting. But like you say, I'd be happy to go home with our current haul.' Her hands tweaked the necklace at her throat. Richard nodded at it.

'That looks good on you.' He meant it. He liked his wife to wear unusual things; beautiful things.

'Thank you for buying it for me. What did you get?' Her hand hadn't left the silver.

'Ah, just a good looking box. I just can't resist them.'

'It's nice. Better a husband who collects boxes than a husband who...' she thought for a moment. 'Plays drums, or something.'

'Ha ha. I suppose so. At least boxes are quiet.'

'And you can put things in boxes.'

'Like other boxes.'

'Yes, quite...'

Contemplative sips. Richard took advantage of the break in conversation and caught the attention of the young barman.

'Hey.' He motioned with his pint glass. 'You wouldn't happen to know why this beer and the pub are both called The Hanged Cat, would you?'

The boy seemed almost startled to be asked the question.

'Well, the beer is named after the pub. The family own a brewery just outside of Milbury.'

'I see. I really like it, by the way.' Richard finished his glass. Lucy was only halfway through her drink, so he motioned for another. 'On the tab please. And why is the pub named the Hanged Cat? It seems a little morbid.'

He became aware that the two men at the bar had not spoken to one another in a while, and appeared to be listening to his own conversation. He gave them a brief nod and turned his attention back to the barman.

The young man shook his head slowly.

'I'm not sure,' he muttered. 'Traditional.'

Richard looked at him quizzically. The boy's discomfort was obvious.

'Man up, Gareth,' said one of the men at the bar. He turned to Richard and Lucy. 'Everyone in Milbury knows why this place is called the Hanged Cat. Are you two staying the night?' Both nodded in the affirmative. 'It may be best not to tell you then. Gareth here has likely been instructed not to relay the tale to anyone taking advantage of the inn's hospitality.'

'A ghost story?' asked Richard. He knew Lucy was an occasional reader of the likes of James, Lovecraft and Poe.

'In kind,' said the man. 'A tale set under this very roof.'

Richard looked at Lucy – she seemed interested – then out the window. A flash of lightning lit a million needles of rain for a split second.

'It's a good night for a ghost story,' said Richard.

Thunder rumbled as the man began.

'This house was not always a pub. The site was originally a Roman villa, or so we like to believe. It's been a hall to the knights of medieval times and a manor for gentry till the days of the Great War. This story takes place in the time they call the Georgian Era.

'A young man, a man named Daniel, had inherited this house upon the death of his father. An estranged branch of the family visited him from a neighbouring county to attend the funeral, and of the dozen relatives who came, one remained with him, a distant cousin.

Daniel took her as his bride.

'Their marriage lasted five years. During this time, the manor prospered. The lord of the house had a stake in the surrounding farmland and the ground yielded as much as it ever had, year after year. The river never dried in summer and never flooded or froze in winter. But Daniel became reclusive, unsociable. There were whispers in the village, rumours started by the maids and servants of the house and grounds. There were things in the house that discomforted visitors – dolls of wicker, candles that burned with strangely coloured flames, and secret locked rooms. All this, and above all, five years of marriage without child.

'They say there came a night in summer when something within Daniel broke. That he took his wife into the grounds of the house, and there hanged her from the fifth-highest branch of the fifth-tallest tree with a length of hempen rope, and when her shuddering corpse had twitched its last the river broke its banks, and the rain didn't stop for five days.'

'Quite a tale,' observed Richard.

'And more to come,' replied the second man. He assumed the narration from his friend.

'Daniel fled the village of Milbury that night. They buried his wife on the third day, in the grounds of the church with the crooked spire. A cross of plain stone was erected above her casket, unmarked. Neither she nor Daniel had visited the church since her arrival half a decade before. There was no service, only a burial. They say her body was as fresh that day as the moment before her death.

'Daniel returned that night with another, a friend and servant, a man they called Stephens. Together they plucked the body from the sodden earth, their task lit only by the watchful eye of the moon. They made to take the body far away, but were halted in their attempt by an outlaw, an agent of fortune. Daniel was slain in the altercation, his body never found, but Stephens was left alive. They found him in the church the next morning, on his knees before the altar, praying that the woman might be dead. They found his carriage some way down the road, burned out from the inside, collapsed, the horses long bolted. The coffin nought but ashes and charred bones inside the blackened shell of the coach.

'Destroying a body will send the soul of a mortal man to heaven. But heaven cannot accommodate those who have forfeited forgiveness, and the soul of a witch is doomed to tread this mortal plane till Judgement Day itself. Brave Daniel was unable to lay his hellish bride to rest before his own passing, and now her uneasy spirit haunts this land, appearing where it may, misleading the lost and tempting the weak, seeking its infernal path back to the world of the living.'

The man paused for effect. The chatter of the other table, the tattoo of rain on the roof and windows, they were somewhere else. The audience was silent in the wake of the story.

'A witch?' said Richard.

The first man nodded.

'The house was examined, of course, since both

its occupants were dead. They found the trappings of her craft in the hitherto forbidden rooms of the manor: heavy tables set in mockery of altars, their cloths mottled with the stains of blood. The hooves and horns of goats. Bottled substances that popped and gave off strange smokes when incinerated. The old church which had accommodated the witch was disavowed, its sanctuary spoiled. The man Stephens died shortly afterwards – to all, it seemed that something inside him simply gave up. The witch's curse, some say. With his death, the rain stopped.'

'Or so the story goes,' said Richard.

'Quite,' replied the man. 'So the story goes.'

'What was her name?' asked Lucy. It was the first time she'd spoken since the story had begun. The second man was the one who answered.

'Elizabeth,' he said. 'May she sleep the slumber of the dead tonight.'

Lightning flashed again and the flames in the hearth bent, as if bowed by some breath of wind. Both men finished their pints. Richard had barely dented his.

'They say she walks the streets of Milbury still, a woman in red, seeking those nearest the threshold of death. For at the instant in which old life departs the mortal shell, new life can slither in. When she wishes to, she takes the form of a black cat with scarlet eyes, the better to remain unnoticed. She casts her influence from beyond the grave, speeding death towards those victims she chooses. To set eyes on her is to look upon the harbinger of your own demise. Always she is searching, grasping and clutching at those ephemeral paths back to the living world.'

Silence fell, and even the rain seemed to slacken in the pause.

'A ghost story, and nothing more,' said the first man. 'I hope it doesn't deprive you of your sleep.'

'I'm sure we'll be fine,' said Richard. He put an arm around Lucy's shoulders as the storm reprised its fury. 'It's just a story, after all.'

* * *

They made love back up in the room. Richard kissed Lucy as the door shut behind them, and slid the zip of her dress down her back slowly. She pulled him to the bed but he took her in his arms and laid her down, sliding himself up her body and pulling both of them under the covers.

* * *

'You haven't taken your necklace off.'

Richard stroked the chain around Lucy's neck.

'I think I might leave it on tonight. It's reassuring having it there. I like wearing the things you buy me, and it's not so big that it will annoy me.'

'I like that.' Richard kissed the base of her throat. He wondered why she needed reassuring.

'Do you like it here?' asked Lucy. Her bedside light had remained on since they'd got back to the room, and she'd made no move to extinguish it before cuddling down against Richard.

'You mean, in Milbury?'

'In this pub, I think.'

Richard stroked the top of her head.

'Did the story upset you? We've stayed in a few haunted hotels before. Remember? We'd spend ages finding good ones and we always used to get disappointed when we didn't have a spooky experience.'

Lucy kissed his chest.

'You're right. I think we usually look into these kinds of places before committing to staying though.' The wind whistled softly up in the roof, as if somewhere in the far distance, a wolf was howling. 'I couldn't mentally prepare myself. And the weather doesn't help.'

'I think we've just had an exciting day. We just need to wind down now and enjoy this night as the little break from reality that it is.' Richard continued to stroke Lucy's hair. She sighed as his thumbs brushed her neck, massaging, and she snuggled in closer to him.

'I wonder what time the bar closes,' murmured Richard. The muted hubbub of voices, the occasional bump and scrape of chairs, filtered through from below. He could feel his wife sliding down into sleep next to him and lent an arm across her, snuffing out the light. She nestled her face in closer but didn't object, didn't seem to waken. Richard closed his own eyes and let himself drift off gently. The room was warm, the wind and rain were a soft rush of sound, elemental and ambient. It had been a long day; the bed was soft. Lucy breathed quietly in her sleep, steady and familiar. Richard dozed, and slipped into sleep.

* * *

Something woke Richard.

The room was dark, but after a few moments his eyes adjusted. A few trees blocked a lamppost outside, but there was still enough light filtering through the blue curtains to illuminate the outlines of shapes in the room. Richard glanced over at Lucy first – she was sleeping on her back, and she looked peaceful. He didn't want to wake her.

He reached gently to the bedside table and tilted his watch toward the available light, but the screen was blank. He tried flicking the buttons on the side, but to no avail: the battery must have died. The watch was cold in his hand, and his gradually wakening mind was puzzled; it had been warm and cosy when he'd nodded off, but outside the duvet it was freezing. It seemed a little cheap to him that the pub would turn the heating off once their guests were asleep.

He'd woken up...

Richard was not a heavy sleeper. He often surfaced from sleep a few times a night; not fully, by any means, but enough to check the time and to nod straight back off again. Sometimes his dreams roused him, but more often a sudden rain or the flailing arm of his wife would jolt him awake. The rain was as heavy now as it had been in the evening and the sounds of the pub crowd sifted through the floor from below.

Milbury folk party hard, thought Richard. He assumed it was the early hours; it was uncommon for him to wake before one in the morning. He laid back and began to peel the thoughts out of his mind, emptying his head to let the sleep back in. He let the prickling sound of rain on glass lull him, and let Lucy's body warm his own. He should drop off any moment now. Any moment...

A cackle rose up from the muted cacophony down at the bar. Richard frowned but in his heart he couldn't blame the crowd downstairs for keeping him awake. Sleep had evaporated from his body, a lost cause. His restless gaze wandered around the room, explored the rafters overhead, the shades-of-black reflection of the mirror, the shivering shadow of the trees on the wall. His mind, always a closet masochist, began to turn towards the least comforting of places – thoughts of unmarked graves, crooked spires and witch's curses. His imagination, quick to decorate these cerebral wanderings with mental images, began seeking out the deepest shadows in the room, drawing shapes into their depths. Richard rolled his eyes at himself. Grow up, mate. Just fiddle with your phone till you're ready to drop off again.

He slipped out from under the covers and hauled himself softly out of the bed. As soon as he'd vacated his spot, Lucy starfished herself across the bed and then reeled the duvet in around her. He'd have to fight her for it when he got back to bed. It really was cold in the room, mind. He placed an experimental hand on the radiator but to his surprise it was hot. When he pulled his hand back even half an inch the heat disappeared. Strange. He fumbled on the floor where his jeans had dropped earlier, wresting his phone from the folds of the pocket. He clicked to illuminate the screen, and saw the time – three in the morning! The bar couldn't still be serving – that would be against the law, surely? He looked again: practically dawn and the pub still sounded alive. He noticed his signal was nil and tried to remember if it had been when they'd arrived. He hadn't really had cause to check his mobile – tried his best not to on weekends away, truth be told.

His mind was properly awake now, and his eyes had adjusted to the darkness. He considered his options. A slice of yellow light glowed under the door from the hall outside. He could go back downstairs. He'd never been at a pub lock-in before. Would Lucy mind? Maybe. He should be ok if he returned before she woke. *Better to regret something you did, than something you didn't do.* He could just go and ask what time they were closing.

He tugged his jeans on. His wallet was still in his pocket – his clothes had been removed with some urgency, and not by him. Shirt next, a little creased from its spell on the floor. Jacket and shoes, the latter left unlaced till he'd stepped out of the room and into the light. He just remembered to grab the room key before closing the door behind him.

The hall was lit by wall lamps with dusty shades. Richard finished tying his laces and padded down the hall. He kept his footfalls light, more out of propriety to the hour than for any real need to keep quiet. The bar sounds were a little easier to discern out here – the sounds of glasses clinking on wood, baritone conversation, quiet folk music. The stairs, encased in a narrow passageway with a low slanted ceiling, creaked beneath his feet. The door into the foyer groaned as he opened it, loudly in the night, the sound of wood and glass and iron hinges being woken from their slumber. As he stepped out from the foyer he realised it was silent in the pub. The bar was empty.

Richard had an active imagination, it was true, but he was a logical man, and down to earth. His practicality, his realism, adapted fast to this unexpected development.

The rain hadn't stopped all night; even now it clattered against the windows and walls. In his waking fancy, the dregs of his sleep had imagined pub sounds mixed into those of the weather. Perhaps the remnants of a dream had whispered to his conscious mind even as he walked down the stairs, more focused on watching his step down the dimly lit flight than on following the sounds of drinking and merriment.

It was still creepy though. Any unfamiliar place is daunting in the dead of night, but a pub is worse, inevitably compared to the place at its most rowdy. The only light came from that same streetlight which had illuminated his bedroom, and much of the space was shadowy and hidden. The conservatory at the far end of the room allowed a little ambient light in but it was too weak to light up the heart of the bar and its dark fireplace.

Lightning flashed and Richard jumped. He shook his head in mockery of himself. *Just a storm, nothing scary. Exciting. Atmospheric. Just enjoy it.* He wandered a little further into the bar. Could he pull himself a pint? He didn't much want one. But should he anyway, for the fun of it?

The fireplace watched him. The hole was very black. Vacuous. It could go on forever. It did, in a way. It led up to the sky, the roof of the world that was no roof at all, no more than a wisp of steam is a lid to a saucepan. The ultimate blackness, the emptiness of space. Richard wondered what the door to hell looked like.

He pressed further, towards the conservatory. He was unnerved, it was true. Things looked different in the dark. Peripheral vision caught columns and hanging coats and turned them to phantoms and reapers. Creaks from the beams above sounded like ghouls, hanging inches behind his head. He pressed a hand against the cold glazing of the conservatory window and stared out into the gardens. A fork of lightning whited out the grounds for a moment before the consequent roll of thunder – the afterimage hung in front of Richard's eyes, a silhouette of shapes in blacks and whites. Was that a twitching figure hanging from the branch of an old tree?

Richard turned away from the window. The lightning flash still blinded his vision but he felt something had changed back inside. He stepped through the tables and chairs, keeping his footfalls as quiet as he could. Had the wraith-like hanging jackets moved? Of course not. He was getting carried away. An overactive imagination on a dark stormy night. He passed the fireplace...

Embers glowed amongst the burned-down wood. They had not been there before in that dark black void. As he watched the glow flared, like the tip of a cigarette brightens when smoked. The phantom cinder seemed to spread, the ash beginning to smoulder. It was like watching a dying fire reverse and resurrect itself. He looked back over to the conservatory –

A white face pressed against the cold, wet glass. Richard jumped in surprise and staggered back into something. He spun round; just a pillar. He looked back at the conservatory. Nothing. The fire had built to a low burn. He could have sworn... A white face: eyes and mouth mere black smudges through the splattered glazing.

No. This was getting ridiculous. It was time to go back to bed. Richard turned his back to the conservatory and to the fireplace. His skin crawled as he imagined that face outside the window; only maybe it was inside now, perhaps even behind him. He shook the feeling away and strode for the stairs, subconsciously keeping his steps silent. He rounded the corner and stopped dead.

Someone was stood opposite him, over in the parlour area. They were staring out of the window, one hand tracing against the lead lattice that webbed across the glass. Richard wondered if they'd seen him, or heard him. He didn't move.

The figure dropped its hand to its jacket, and consulted a pocket watch. It turned from the window and Richard could see it was a man, though its form was indistinct; blurry. The stranger seemed to be looking in his direction but didn't seem to register his presence. It began to walk towards him.

Richard's stomach plummeted in his body. If this was some entity, some ghost, let it pass by him. Let it keep walking on its own plane, oblivious to mortal distractions. Richard felt the terror of the surreal, the supernatural, of nightmares. The figure, its eyes staring at some other unseen thing, halted before Richard. Then it looked at him.

Richard felt blank. There are different aspects of fear, different forms it can take. What Richard felt now was the terror of unknowing. He knew not what stood before him, not what it could do. Where it had come from, why it had come. He could only stare at it, numb.

'Richard...'

It spoke like a man but its voice was somehow hollow, as if the vocal cords that had produced the sound waves weren't really there.

'Richard...' The stranger's hands were raised as if to take Richard by the throat. The threat of immediate danger connected to something in his brain and Richard stepped back, a stumble at first, then faster, backing away till he hit the bar and could retreat no further. The thing opposite him advanced. It moved unnaturally, almost gliding, as if the movements of its legs were superfluous, mere ornament to its true means of ambulation. Its eyes were dead and staring but they could see, yes, because they were looking at him, through him. Richard could not shut his own eyes, could not even blink. His hands bit into the counter at his back. The thing halted before him, and its grasping ghostly hands began to curl forwards.

* * *

Lucy rolled over in bed. She slept, but part of her realised it was cold, and she pulled the covers in around her, rolling into them. Part of her, too, recognised that Richard was gone. She didn't think too much of it: Richard was a light sleeper, and often rose for short spells at night. Lucy's sleeping mind gauged no threat, and allowed her to sleep on.

* * *

The ghost, if that's what it was, paused before its claws could fix around Richard's throat. It held its hands together as if in prayer or pleading, and its mouth cracked open as it rasped:

'Richard... You must help me...'

Its clasped hands overlapped slightly, one fading into the other. It made no effort to touch Richard, or to cause him distress. Its countenance was one of concern and dread; perhaps this is what eased Richard's own fright, if but a little. It looked scared itself.

'You are Richard, yes..?' the ghost enquired. Its voice was becoming firmer, less gasping, but Richard still fancied that the words it spoke did not come from its mouth any more than the ghost's feet touched the floor. The sound wave of its voice, the acoustic vibration, just began at a point within the slightly translucent shape in front of him. As to its feet, they appeared to sink half an inch into the stone tiles, as if resting on some other floor that used to exist a long time ago.

The ghost continued to stare, its eyeballs like ghastly baubles. Its expression was imploring. Richard recalled its question. He nodded, slowly, identifying himself. He didn't believe the spirit meant him harm, and didn't know what harm it could do to him even if it wanted to. What scared him most was the *wrongness* of the apparition; by all accounts a ghost is a dead thing, and to see a dead thing animated and speaking shattered some fundamental understanding with nature that Richard held inside himself. His nod was not so much a reply to the ghost as it was a response to the incitement of conversation – something familiar, something normal in such an abnormal situation. He nodded slowly again, an affirmative hushing somewhere under his breath, still reluctant to emerge as sound.

The ghost bowed its head in answer, and spoke with a voice still less hoarse and faltering than before.

'Then I bid you welcome, Richard, to my house. You have journeyed far to arrive here, and will travel further still before this night is done. Your coming heralds an end: an end to deathly wandering and to a timeless abhorrence. You are the release, Richard, the salvation.' It paused for a moment. Richard could see through its semi-solid form to the darkness behind, lit for a split second by a crack of lightning. The ghost's blue lips opened again. 'My name is Daniel.'

Daniel. The lord of the manor. Richard remembered the tale. Daniel had indeed been slain some two hundred years ago, murdered on the road out of Milbury by a thief. *After murdering his wife*, he recalled. *After stringing her up and leaving her to choke and die.* He made to speak, but managed only a whisper.

'Why are you here?'

Addressing the phantom seemed to reinforce the notion of its presence, and a fresh drip of fear slithered down Richard's body.

'We have always been here,' the ghost replied. 'Since death refused to take us and hell itself spat us back into the world.'

The fear in Richard's gut coiled like weeds. For the first time, the ghost smiled. Its words were slow but clear.

'My apologies, Richard. It becomes harder to choose one's words with care when one is a creature of darkness. It is harder to distinguish between good and evil when one exists beyond their very concept.'

'You killed your wife.'

'I tried.' The ghoulish smile was gone: now it wore a frown of disquiet and fear. 'For the good of everything I held dear I tried. But the witch's skill was formidable, her will to survive unquenchable. The grave could never claim her; I am no true murderer.'

'Then why are you here?' Richard kept his voice

low, as if on some unconscious level he did not want to be found conversing with a dead man. His hands still held onto the wooden worktop of the bar behind him as if anchoring him to familiarity.

'As I said, Richard,' answered the ghost. Its pallid expression grew sterner still. 'To end this restless purgatory. To complete the task which, left unfinished, has surely barred my crossing from this world to the next. To arrest the spirit of the Milbury Witch, and then to destroy it.'

Silence fell.

Richard felt overwhelmed. Part of him still believed this encounter was a figment of his imagination, some gravely misunderstood shred of nightmare he had carried with him from his bed. To give consideration to the words of the ghost gave substantiation to its existence, and he was reluctant to do even this. However, with the inclination of a dream, he played along. His pragmatism accepted the situation — *if this is a dream, then speaking to a ghost is only natural. If this is real... The ghost believes in you. Maybe it's time to believe in it, too* — and he asked the most rational of questions.

'Why me?' he said. He hated the way it sounded, as if he'd picked up from a made-for-television film, and he elaborated. 'I'd never heard of Milbury till today. We never planned to visit. We have nothing to do with this... this situation.'

'Nor do any who stumble into such things,' remarked the phantom. Its voice seemed, for the first time since it had spoken, wistful. 'There are forces in this world of whose existence we are given no indication — until, that is, their paths converge with ours. Your path has led you here this night. You, Richard... You do not matter. You could have been anyone. But it is here, on this night, that forces are stirring. You have felt them, heard them. The echoes of the past rattle plainly for those inclined to hear them.'

'I was in the wrong place at the wrong time.'

'You are in this place, at a time when things that have lain dormant have begun to wake. After centuries of incarceration on this plane, there rises now an opportunity for me to rid this world of the vengeful spirit of Elizabeth, and in doing so, allow me to break free of my cursed existence and earn my place on the other side.'

The ghost stared at Richard – at least, its eyes pointed towards him. Richard still wasn't sure whether the thing before him was the shadow of a man or some kind of puppet; a physical aspect projected by the incomprehensible entity that was an undead soul. Richard sensed that the ghost was awaiting a reply.

'What do you need me to do?' he asked. With any luck the thing would evaporate into the ether before it required him to do anything. That is, if Richard didn't wake up, or at least come to his senses, first.

'You are mortal, Richard.' The ghost smiled again. 'You may act upon this world in a way that my kind cannot. It is you that must perform the rites that will deliver the witch's spirit from this world.'

'I can't do that. I don't know how.'

'You will play your part, Richard. Those forces that grant me animation will surely grant you the knowledge to execute these ceremonies.'

'I don't...' The mind will only indulge so much disbelief. Richard's was reaching its limit. 'I don't want to.

I don't want to have to do this. I don't want this to happen to me.'

The ghost frowned again, its face pleading.

'You must, Richard. Remember: you are my salvation.' It seemed to flicker for a moment. Richard wondered if he'd imagined this. 'Come. Walk with me. Let me show you through my house.'

* * *

Lucy rolled into a cold patch in the bed. She woke, a little, dimly. She noticed Richard's absence, and then recalled the first time she'd half-woken in the empty bed. Her eyes flickered open.

Richard was gone. Yes. She sat up and looked around. It was dark, but not so dark that she couldn't make out the outlines of objects in the room, and a growing sense of worry gnawed at the pit of her stomach. She peered through the open bathroom door but could not see her husband in there. Checking the time on her wristwatch – three in the morning – she realised the tiny hands had ceased to move. It must have run down its battery, maybe even at three in the afternoon. She wouldn't have noticed. At any rate, she felt Richard had been gone for some time. Some instinct flared in her gut and she knew she couldn't go back to sleep now.

Lucy eyed the slit of yellow light beneath the door. She would go and find her husband.

* * *

Daniel's ghost led Richard up the stairs. They seemed darker now than when he had descended them earlier that night. He'd been alone then, following the sounds of life below. In a way, he supposed, he was still alone. Wooden beams arched over his head and he noticed that, where lights had perched before, candle sconces were fixed into the walls. As they reached the top, Richard recognised the shape of the corridor. He spied the door to his own rented room, but knew on some level that Lucy was not sleeping peacefully behind it. He was in something of the ghost's own world now.

Daniel led him on down the corridor, passing Richard's room. There was a door at the end of the corridor and it swung open as they approached, smoothly and without a sound. Daniel paused before it. Richard wondered whether he would simply pass through the spectre if he didn't stop walking, and what it would feel like. Unpleasant, no doubt. Cold.

It seemed almost like Daniel was waiting, preparing himself for some signal to enter. If such a signal was given, Richard didn't notice it, and the ghost stepped over the threshold. Richard followed him in.

It was a bedroom. Richard felt sure he was exploring the past now: the room was lit by candles mounted on a hanging candelabrum, and the four poster bed looked old-fashioned but fresh – a recently made relic. The curtains were drawn around it. Richard noticed it was still raining outside – tiny rivers trickled down the windowpanes – but the sound was reduced, as if he were hearing it from a long way away.

'I first met Elizabeth in the springtime, in the year of our lord seventeen fifty-nine,' Daniel's spirit intoned.

'It was at the funeral of my father. He was interred not far from here, at the church of the twisted spire.'

'I know it,' said Richard.

The ghost carried on as if he hadn't heard.

'The branches of my family had been estranged for many years: the civil war of a century before had divided kin as well as country. The death of a patriarch was an opportunity for us to convene as acquaintances, if not as relatives. Elizabeth's family travelled for two days to attend the funeral.' The ghost creased his icy brow. 'A stilted reunion, if well-intentioned. One cannot affect fondness for those he has never met before, especially in such dismal circumstances.'

'But you met your wife.'

'Yes.' A mix of emotion seemed to cross the spirit's face. 'I met Elizabeth. A quiet soul, her appearance pleasing in my eyes. If I had known…' his voice trailed off.

Richard gave the ghost a minute to compose himself. He looked around the bedroom. The candles cast a yellow light about the space that left much in cold black shadow. The walls were thinly papered, and the rain-veined windows were given scant comfort by long hanging curtains. A richly carved wardrobe and dresser hinted at wealth. The mirror above the dresser gave no reflection of Richard or his guide. Richard turned as Daniel resumed his story. His voice now had a determined edge to it.

'Elizabeth gave me sympathy that night. She cast her first spell upon me here.' Daniel pointed to the bed. Richard could see the shadow of movement behind the curtains; hear the rustle of covers as the two of them communed, comforting each other physically. He did not know if he was witnessing something from the past or some spectral re-enactment. He felt uncomfortable, voyeuristic, but he wondered whether he was really seeing this act at all. The atmosphere of the ghost world could simply be affecting him, encouraging him to dream out the visuals of the story.

'At first her magic was harmless. She bound my affections to her, compelled me to love her. A victim of her craft, I knew nothing different. I did love her.' Lightning flashed outside the window, and the sky lit up for as long as five seconds, as if time itself were being stretched, or was simply wrong. 'Elizabeth stayed with me when her kin returned to their town across the plains. We lived here, in this house, accompanied only by the servants. They would whisper that we lived in sin, though our chambers were kept separate. After a time, we wed, and the whispers stopped for a while.'

Richard felt himself envisaging the scene – a small ceremony, performed on a spring afternoon, under the shadow of a warped steeple and the watchful eye of a father's grave.

'We kept our own chambers out of habit, as man keeps his study his own. We slept together here every night however, the masters of the house. By day I tended to my affairs about the area. The farmland yielded well under my leadership and I cultivated strong friendships with my staff. But as I worked, so did Elizabeth.'

Daniel beckoned to Richard.

'Follow me.'

He led Richard back through the bedroom door and into the corridor, the spine of the house. They appeared to be making for the stairs, but Daniel stopped at the top of the flight without acknowledging it at all. Instead, he faced the blank wall in front of him.

'You understand, Richard, that we now inhabit a world of shadows. We are no longer conforming to the architecture of this house as you know it.'

'Yes. Though I don't understand how.'

'The west wing of the house was boarded away some time ago.' The ghost paid no heed to Richard's doubtful remark. 'I saw men come in carrying tools and timbers, and watched them barricade the old doors, the old halls. There is more to this building than first appearance may show.'

Richard understood what the ghost was insinuating.

'I can't walk through walls,' he remonstrated. 'I'm mortal. It's liable to hurt.'

'You must believe, Richard,' Daniel insisted. His face was warmer now, kinder. His lips seemed less blue and his form, though still transparent, did not seem to be clutching to remain corporeal. 'Have I not shown you that there is more in heaven and earth than you have previously dreamt of?'

'You have. It has not always made me comfortable.'

'A little more belief, friend,' implored the ghost. 'Come with me. Step through the door.'

Now Richard looked closely, it did seem as if there was a door impressed into the wall. Some shadow behind the plaster, like the dark shape of a whale seen from above water. Daniel smiled at Richard reassuringly, and stepped through the wall.

For a moment Richard was alone – truly alone.

His mind turned to escape, and he looked down the stairs in momentary hope. They were bottomless, steps upon steps leading down forever, until they faded into blackness. He looked back down the corridor to his room, but there was no escape available there either. If Lucy were here he would feel her, and he could not. He was on another plane now, a plane where all corridors led to infinity and all doors opened into the void.

He looked back at the wall and tried to visualise that door. He closed his eyes and imagined it there in front of him: a dark wood frame and a panelled leaf swung back to admit him, like the open pages of a book invite a reader. He took a deep breath and extended his hand. There was something there, to be sure, but it didn't stop his hand's progress. He inched his feet forwards and a feeling grew along his arm, a feeling like seizing-up muscles. His fingers, however, now felt fine.

His creeping feet took a small, tentative step, and he felt the cramping sensation envelop his body. It was surreal, as if his innards were tensing at the touch of unseen boards. It was uncomfortable and he forced himself through the sensation. It was strongest along his vertical axis and he imagined his body pushing through some central timber mullion, his atoms aligning against those in the wood by some supernatural quantum mechanics, allowing both to exist in tandem with the other. Then the feeling was gone, as if it had never been. Richard opened his eyes.

* * *

Lucy hauled on some clothes beneath the dim overhead bulb. She was sure she would find Richard downstairs somewhere, though where he had gone to she had no idea. *He may just be exploring*, she thought to herself. For such a down-to-earth man, he did get fanciful ideas in his head sometimes. She couldn't shake the feeling that there was someone else here though. *Of course there must be*, she reasoned. The manager must live on the premises. Unless he just lived next-door, or nearby? She wasn't sure how these things worked. She remembered the manager telling herself and Richard that they were the only guests tonight but still, she felt a presence, as if other people were around in the house somewhere.

She searched for the room key – a shiny modern Yale attached to a lumpy strip of wood – but couldn't find it anywhere. As she looked on Richard's bedside table, she noticed that his watch had stopped too: the small grey digital display was perfectly blank. The fear and concern that had haunted her as she fell asleep began to resume their work and she attempted to rationalise the coincidence. It worried her more as a symptom, a manifestation of something dark, than because a stopped watch is scary in itself. She'd watched a film once where everyone's watches had stopped before an alien invasion; something to do with electromagnetic waves. She knew there wasn't going to be an alien invasion but she supposed all the lightning might have disrupted something in the electrics. *Of your analogue watch?* she questioned herself. She pushed the logical snag to the back of her mind. It didn't matter anyway. Richard mattered.

She couldn't find the room key – Richard must have taken it – and instead pocketed her dead phone as well as her house keys. Just in case. The door didn't have a latch so she was forced to leave it ajar, propped open with an upturned cup from the tray of teas left on the dresser. She made sure the cup was wedged securely and that the door was lodged open before rising to her feet and making for the stairs. There was a creak from behind her and she twisted violently – her nerves, she realised for the first time, on edge. But there was no one at her back.

Lucy shook off the twinge of fear and cocked her head at the darkness. She'd been drawn to the ground floor because that's where she and her husband had come from. But Richard might be exploring further into the house. She padded forwards. The hallway lights illuminated the corridor with a pale electric glow, but the light petered out further down the hall. She passed her own room. There was a doorway dead ahead and a turning to the left that she could not see around. As she stepped closer, she became aware of a scraping sound, rhythmic, coming from behind the corner. The corridor seemed to stretch on forever, as if her steps were in slow motion. She began to feel a sense of impending fear, as in a dream.

Strange, she thought to herself, unbidden. *In a nightmare, you know when something scary is about to happen, because your brain is the thing that fabricates it in the first place. So why do we keep dreaming? Why do we invite the terror? And if we invent it ourselves, why is it still frightening?*

The scraping continued, a rasping, scratching, chafing sound, and Lucy took a deep breath as if she were about to plunge into water. She could see that there were no lights glowing behind the corner. The lamps behind her flickered on and off with an electric humming noise and she shivered inside.

Scrape. Scrape. Scrape.

All rational thought had abandoned her now, and she remembered the Milbury Witch who had lived here within these very walls. Had she chalked symbols and spells into floorboards and walls – *scrape* – or ground down the bones of creatures to dust – *scrape* – to use in her witchcraft?

She rounded the corner, the hall before her lit with moonlight from the lead-latticed window and bordered with dark wooden beams. There was a figure down that corridor, its back to Lucy. It hunched as it worked, running a pair of skeletal, battered broomsticks over the floor. *Scrape. Scrape.* Lucy breathed in relief. A cleaner. That's all.

The figure stiffened as it became aware of an audience. It pulled itself upright. There was something unnatural in its movement, as if it had no joints. It turned around, but Lucy could not see a face – it stood beyond the halo of moonlight cast by the window. One of the broomsticks edged into the light and the figure shuffled forwards – *scrape* – its brooms like crutches, its legs stiff and ungainly. Lucy's breath caught in a stunted scream as the figure stepped into the light.

Its face was like leather, creased and woody, and its expression was fixed, blank, inhuman. Its coat was torn, a scarecrow's jacket, and Lucy saw with horror that it wasn't holding the broomsticks; they protruded from the sleeves of the coat – they were its arms. As it shambled forwards fragments fell from beneath its clothes, pieces of straw, and the broomsticks swept at the strands, kicking them into a tiny dusty blizzard.

Her lungs wouldn't work but Lucy's legs could – just. She twisted, moving as if through treacle, as if in a dream, pointing herself back down the corridor she'd come from, conscious always of the dreadful rasp of the creature's gait, terrified that its reaching twig fingers might prickle her back or wrap chafingly around her legs. She pushed herself on, the effort unbelievable, the woody scratching of the sticks rasping ever louder in her ears as she waded forwards and away from her pursuer. The more she pushed the easier it became till she was running, really running, and the world was light again and she skidded to a halt before crashing into the blank wall ahead of her. She threw herself around to check for the creature that had chased her but there was nothing. No sound but the bass throb of blood pumping in her ears.

The corridor seemed more in focus now, more real. The light from the electric lamps lit the space with a yellow synthetic glow, revealing nothing of a pursuer, and yet Lucy could hardly believe she'd woken from some ghost story-inspired night-terror. She felt the hard jab of her car keys in her pocket and the presence of something so mundane helped calm her, ground her in reality, but even so... She'd never dreamt something so vivid, so terrifying. She edged forwards, half expecting the walls to warp and lengthen as they bent to admit that stick-creature from another supernatural dimension. They did not. She walked as far as the corner and peeked around, seeing nothing but blank space. No floorboards either – carpet. No need for broomsticks then. She tried the door opposite her, the one in sight of her own bedroom. It was locked. She was relieved. If it was locked it meant Richard couldn't be in there. And that nothing could get out. She considered calling anyway, just in case, but found she wasn't able to make any more than a quiet croak. Her encounter, imaginary or not, had shaken her.

'Lucy,' she whispered to herself, in a voice so low she herself could barely sense it. 'We're searching for Richard. Richard.' She emphasised her husband's name, let it strengthen her. Assured now that she could still articulate if required to do so, she stepped onwards down the corridor. As she passed the patch of moonlight she couldn't suppress a shiver. Something had stood here, even if it had existed only in her mind.

There was one more door at the end of this passage; it loomed ahead of her like the end of a tunnel. A flash of recent memory: twig nails scratching at rough floorboards and a leathery face carved from impassive wood. Lucy pushed the image away and marched up to the door, pausing for a moment to listen for any sounds behind it. Satisfied there were none, she tried the handle. A clunk as the bolt rattled stubbornly in its mortise. Good. Now that the top floor was cleared, Lucy could go find Richard downstairs.

As she passed her bedroom she peeked inside. It was empty – *as well it should be*, she thought – and the sight of it filled her with a curious fortitude. It was her room, her space, if only for the night, and it was her sanctuary if she needed it. Nothing could come in unless she admitted it, and if she needed a place to secrete herself then she could do it here. Her safe place.

Lucy reached the top of the stairs. They seemed somewhat steeper than she'd been aware of previously. She hadn't noticed the lack of bannister before either, and she was obliged to place a hand on the cold wall to steady herself as she descended. She reckoned she could hear sounds below; hushed voices and quiet movement, and she told herself it was Richard, talking to that irritable old manager. She kept her footsteps quiet, in case it wasn't.

The sounds became clearer as she neared the door at the bottom of the stairs. She glanced back up to the landing but there was nothing following her. The light up there seemed changed, though; it was softer, with a wavering movement to it. Shaking her head and returning her attention to the door before her, Lucy peeked through the glass panels. She could discern the movement of figures through the frosted panes and, not wishing to appear strange for lurking, opened the door with affected confidence.

There was a crowd collected in the parlour area, some two dozen men and women. They wore old-fashioned clothes and were all dressed in black. They reminded Lucy of a flock of vultures, and she wondered what they were doing here in the dead of night. Their presence made her uneasy. Though the door had creaked like a coffin lid when she'd opened it, none of the throng had yet acknowledged her. She did not move from her spot by the door.

When the figures spoke to each other they did so in whispers, and Lucy could not discern the words they hissed. She began to fear them. There was a table arranged with platters of food but no one seemed to be touching it. If a face turned towards her, it did not appear to notice her, and would turn back to one of its fellows in due course.

Lucy assumed they were ghosts. It seemed to make sense to her – she supposed that, like the scent of perfume can linger in the air after its wearer has gone, so too could the echoes of the past resonate in the present. Once she had decided this, rationalised it to herself, her fear shrank and she stepped forwards. None of the party looked at her. She guessed that the creature upstairs, the broomstick construct, had been an echo too. That one had noticed her, though. Or had it? Perhaps she had appeared to it as the black-clad crowd appeared to her now. Perhaps it had simply spotted some sign of another world and clawed at it, its appearance muddled and morphed through the prism of the centuries as it rushed towards something strange and incredible.

An unsettling thought occurred to Lucy. If she had stumbled into this supernatural place, this junction in time, then perhaps Richard had too. An icicle of sudden dread pierced her soul as the implication hit her, and she hoped to God that he had not slipped somewhere with no way to return.

'No,' she whispered to herself. 'Keep looking. Find Richard.'

Lucy realised the room was lit by candles and coals, the latter clumped in braziers bolted into the walls, rather than the electric lights of the evening. Watching the subdued (and slightly blurry) faces of the dark ghosts, she realised they must be a funeral party. Glancing round, she saw the restaurant was no longer inhabited by a host of tables and chairs but furnished with low wooden benches and hanging tapestries. The bar still clung to the nearside wall though, and Lucy understood she was experiencing some form of convergence where all things existed in parallel. The rain still beat at the windows and she wondered whether it was from her own time or whether it had been raining on the night of the wake.

Beneath the noise of the downpour Lucy detected another sound coming from outside. It was a low knocking, irregular, quiet. The funeral party did not acknowledge it. She strained her ears to make out the source of the sound. It disquieted her; it was like the scratching of the stick creature. Something that might not exist but that might hurt her if it did. It seemed to be coming from behind the front door. Lucy crept towards it.

The door had not changed. Perhaps it had remained intact through the years, or maybe it was, like the bar, a piece of the present that had lingered on. The knocking sound came from the other side, low down, a muffled bumping. Lucy was within two feet of the door. The sound made her think of a vessel bobbing in rough waters, colliding intermittently with a pier. After a moment, she realised it had stopped.

Lucy peered at the door, suspicious. Something as innocent as a branch caught in the wind, or a passing animal pawing at the door? She supposed it had sounded like a small creature pleading entry, but it seemed unlikely on such a night. She realised she was bending down to listen to the sound, and straightened. As she did, there came a fully-fledged couplet of knocks at the door, bold and clear. Lucy jumped out of her skin. The door seemed to loom bigger than it had a moment before, now that it was the portal to some threatening danger. Lucy was frozen to the spot. Two more knocks reverberated through the oak, through Lucy. The funeral party could not hear them. They were meant for her. She felt like she and the door were the only things in existence, two entities on a pedestal surrounded by empty space. A fifth and final knock on the door: the sound of ancient Celtic iron ramming into weather-beaten oak. Lucy moved as if under a spell. What choice did she have? She was a pawn in a supernatural design; she must do what she was bidden.

The iron handle was heavy in her hand, but Lucy heaved, and the bolt inside the door grated back with all the weighty purpose of an eternal pendulum. The door rolled inwards, and Lucy stepped back to avoid its path. She looked up to see a figure, garbed in red, obscured by the darkness of the night. Rain shone on its dark crimson form and Lucy instinctively backed away, shaking herself free of the spell that had compelled her for a minute. A blaze of lightning illuminated the world for a split second and, in that moment, Lucy beheld the Milbury Witch.

* * *

The room was dark. Pitch dark. Richard blinked hard, checking that his eyes were indeed open.

'Daniel.' Richard groped around him, scared suddenly of the most simple of terrors. 'I can't see.' His hands felt the solid wall behind him, the solid wall he'd just passed through, and the contact with unmoving board and plaster cued a thrill of fear to rattle through him. He kept his voice from pleading, but begged his guide for aid. 'Daniel. Help, please...'

When he looked back around there was a faint green glow. It grew stronger and Richard realised it was a small emerald fire, held in the ghost's right hand. Daniel nodded at him.

'My apologies Richard. Some things do not travel

through the gulf of time intact, and my kind do not notice the lack of light. I would not wish you to despair.'

Richard realised that he found the sight of a ghost grasping a handful of flames of more comfort to him than the dark. This revelation did not wholly reassure him. As he watched, the fire grew and flowed, filling the room with a dim verdigris ambience.

'We are in the witch's quarters now,' murmured Daniel. A flicker of fire remained in his hand like a lantern. 'Tread carefully. Echoes can live on through the years; we do not know what may dwell here.'

Richard glanced around him. The room was an entrance chamber of sorts; the door to a house within a house. It was small, sparsely furnished with a low dressing table. Three doors led off further into the deeper bowels of the place. Daniel glided to the first and took the handle with his fiery hand. After he'd turned it and opened the door, the handle remained green, as if rusted. Daniel beckoned Richard closer, letting the fire light the place. Richard stepped through the door.

'The first of her chambers,' whispered Daniel. 'Behold the trappings of her craft.'

There were no windows in the tiny room; it was little more than a cupboard. The green fire cast a sickly pallor in the space, picking out objects arranged neatly on shelves and dressing tables. An iron cauldron rested ahead of them, a sheaf of twigs and herbs propped up inside it. Around it myriad items rested – dull bells of various sizes, scissors, goblets. Wicker dolls lay like tiny stiff corpses, their limbs stuck out like stars. Richard could smell something too, a musky fragrance that had seeped through centuries. It reminded him of incense and old stale houses.

'She performed magic here?' asked Richard. He realised he been envisioning something more akin to a Halloween crone in a pointed hat than a real witch; what he supposed a Wiccan must be.

'Some,' affirmed the ghost. 'But not the darkest of what she was capable. I chanced more than once to find this door unlocked, just as the servants must have whilst about their household duties. There was always something of the other world about Elizabeth; she could be found even in plain sight twisting lengths of corn into effigies and burning curious candles. The village cats often sought her out and followed her about the house and grounds. But the items found here only confirmed her affinity with the old folk ways. They suggested nothing deeper, nothing of the black spells she had cast against me. Against this village.'

Richard frowned at Daniel. He supposed that if he was speaking to a ghost, then magic and spells could exist in the world too. He wondered if the supernatural world conformed to its own branch of science. The ghost continued to speak.

'Over time I became convinced of Elizabeth's nature. The love-charm she wove around me would wear thin on occasion, if only for a few hours, and I began to guess at what she had done. Each time the spell resumed its hold, it was weaker, and at last there came a day when I realised I was free. I no longer loved her. She had deceived me.'

Daniel led Richard from the witch's cell and closed the door behind them. He paused before the second door.

'The servants had good reason to whisper,' he acknowledged. 'Elizabeth and I had been wed for four years and never had she displayed a mark of pregnancy. As her influence over me slipped I realised the truth: that her pact with the devil had prevented her from bearing a child.' The green fire in Daniel's hand flared and shaped itself into the semblance of a key – he slid it into the old lock and twisted. Richard pictured the internal workings of the lock tumbling and sliding under the unnatural flame, or perhaps just burning away entirely. Daniel retrieved the key and pushed at the second door.

'This door was always locked whilst Elizabeth lived here. In my spellbound state I allowed her this privacy, oblivious to her true nature or to the real purpose of this chamber. Richard: witness the darkest incarnation of witchcraft.'

The door swung inwards and Daniel entered, beckoning Richard to follow. This room was larger, the size of a study or a small bedroom. A window administered an icing of moonlight to the scene, mixing with the absinthe glow of Daniel's ghost-light. Richard hesitantly crossed the threshold and entered the heart of the witch's lair.

A table was poised against the back wall, low and covered with a dark red cloth, resembling a church altar. Thick black candles were arranged across its back like spires. Daniel advanced further into the room and Richard saw the floor had been chalked with a large pentacle, the star at its centre large enough for a body to stand in.

Shelves against one wall displayed jars and stacks of leather-bound books, and what looked worryingly like animal bones and hooves. Daniel lit the candles on the table with his fire and they illuminated the objects atop the altar with their otherworldly light. Richard stepped forward in spite of himself, his curiosity overruling his trepidation. The altar top was more visible now, bathed in green, and he saw a goat's skull had been arranged at its centre, iron daggers placed on either side. The empty eye sockets gazed out at the unhallowed scene, plumes of white smoke rising from the candles on either side, casting a heavy, claustrophobic scent through the room.

'The witch's chamber,' announced Daniel. The ghost seemed triumphant, as if proud to prove his wife's guilt. 'It was here that Elizabeth paid homage to her dark masters, and here that they rewarded her with knowledge of the black arts. It was here that she constructed a mask of beauty to beguile our neighbours and here that she cast the spells necessary for her wealth and success.'

Richard was speechless. The scene was like something from a horror film but dreadful in its authenticity. He looked down at the old floorboards and saw discolourations, as if something dark had been spilled there. He gazed into the eye-hollows of the horned skull on the altar and shuddered at the implication.

'You have seen enough, Richard?' enquired his guide. Richard stared around the chamber once more, transfixed by the horrific sights. He nodded slowly. 'Then come. Follow me.'

Daniel extended an arm, gently ushering Richard from the room. The air seemed clearer out in the entrance chamber. Daniel shut the door behind him.

'Come with me. We will find relative sanctuary in here.'

The spirit opened the third and final door and strode boldly in. Richard followed with an apprehension that eased upon seeing the comparative normality of the room – a bedchamber, like the one Daniel had shown him earlier. He perceived that Daniel's form was now as distinct as his own, and commented on it. Daniel turned and nodded.

'We are closer to my world now than when we first met. It is easier to manifest a solid form due to this proximity.'

Richard nodded, and in doing so noticed his own appearance had taken on something of a disembodied quality.

'Am I becoming a ghost, Daniel?' His voice wavered, the thought compounding the sense of unease he'd felt since entering the witch's chamber. He held up a slightly translucent hand to show his guide.

'No, Richard. Just as my form altered upon entering your plane, so yours is adapting to my own world, a world of echoes and memory. Your rightful, corporeal form will restore itself as we return to the mortal plane.'

The spirit's explanation seemed to make sense, and satisfied Richard's pragmatic mind. The bedroom was quiet and he felt as if a great roaring in his ears had stopped, though he hadn't noticed any sound in the other room. He could feel the presence of the chamber even now, conscious that it lurked on the other side of the wall. Daniel bade him sit on an old chair beside a window. Outside, the rain pattered down in slow motion, like viscous tears. Daniel parted the curtains of the four-poster bed and seated himself on the edge. He leaned forwards.

'Thank you Richard,' he started. 'You have seen many dark things tonight. Things that have no doubt disturbed you. You've shown great fortitude. I ask only for a little more.' Richard became aware of how weak he felt, how drained. He had a mild headache and guessed that crossing spectral boundaries hadn't fully agreed with him. Daniel was still speaking. 'There is a little more of my story. A small amount that you must hear before we combat the witch. You must hear of the night I slew Elizabeth.'

A slow flash of lightning and a long peal of thunder. Richard closed his eyes and let the visions come to him.

'On that fateful night, it numbered five years to the day since I first set eyes on Elizabeth. As I told you, I had broken free of her spells, and the previous day had forced entry to her locked cell whilst she was about the village. What I found shocked and appalled me as surely as it horrified you, and I knew I must act. I studied the volumes I found in her chamber and spent the next day gathering the instruments I would require to slay the witch.

'On the evening of the fifth of May, I advanced silently on Elizabeth as she gathered herbs and grasses from the garden. She was alerted to my approach by her dark craft and saw that I knew her secret. We fell to fighting, her strength unnatural for a woman of her stature. I remember that neither of us spoke a word, nor cried out at all. She seized a knife from the ground and made to murder me, but I wrested it from her and slipped a noose of hempen rope around her neck. She twisted and writhed in my arms as I dragged her to a yew tree and threw the rope over the gallows branch. As I hauled her higher she began to shudder violently and grow smaller: she took on the form of a black cat with bloody red eyes. But the rope slid tighter, weighted by her own body, and the cat became as trapped as she. As her life failed she turned back to her womanly form, her neck broken by the tight bonds. I watched her twitch her last, her body spinning back and forth from that branch. But my work was not complete.

'The witch's spirit is bound to its mortal form in life, but can break free following death. The two must be united for both the body and soul to be laid to rest. I planned to cut the corpse from the tree and remove it in order to perform these ceremonies, but was interrupted in my work by the attentions of the villagers. Two illicit lovers on a nocturnal venture chanced to see the body swinging from the tree and raised the alarm. I fled, fearing the persecution of my uncomprehending neighbours, and hid in the nearby woods.

'I was cold and the rain never ceased; I would have been unable to defend myself if found. I heard the search parties the following day and attempted to hide, but one man found me: Stephens, a servant on my estate, a man I called a friend before Elizabeth's devilment drove me to distraction. I convinced him to keep my whereabouts a secret, and to bring me aid. He like as not saved my life, bringing me food and dry clothes. Further still, he brought me information the next day – that Elizabeth was considered a victim of my murderous intentions, and was to be buried in hallowed ground at the church of the crooked spire. That the witch was to lie in the same sacred ground as my father I could not abide. I conspired with my friend Stephens to disinter her body the next night and remove her to a site of ancient magic, the stone circle across the plains. Once there, I would fix the witch to her coffin with five silver nails – one through each hand and foot and a final drawn through her mouth – to bind her spirit and body together. Silver is anathema to the witch, and burying her in a web of ancient magic would prevent her soul from ever rising again.'

Richard remembered the story he had been told earlier that night – an evening that seemed so very far in the past.

'You were stopped,' he recalled. 'Stopped by a highwayman.'

Daniel nodded and his face darkened in anger.

'Stephens commissioned a gun, a coach and horses, and met me at the church. We dug the casket from the ground as quickly and quietly as we could, and began our journey to the witch's final resting place. Our journey was laborious, the road drenched from days of rain. The thief ran us down easily – we were not fighting men, we could not defend ourselves. He murdered me in cold blood and left me dying on the roadside. I watched as he plundered and lusted over Elizabeth's body, for even in death she held her devil-bestowed beauty. He rode away into the night with his slim spoils, leaving me for dead. Stephens failed to find me in the dark and was forced to improvise. He made a pyre of the coach and burned the witch's corpse. I saw the first tongues of flame and cursed his folly before the darkness overwhelmed me.'

The ghost's face was glaring, ugly with the memories of death and failure. Richard considered consoling him.

'When did you return as...' he paused. Daniel looked up.

'A ghost?' he spat. 'Less than a week later. They never found my body, or so I heard. I can only imagine that Stephens found it by the light of the fire and threw it in with the witch. Perhaps he feared being branded a murderer. I awoke on that lonely road next to a blackened patch of grass and stone and made my return to the village. I had no form, I was simply...' he felt for the right word. 'An existence. I merely thought about direction to move; I had no body to animate. I returned to my house and found I could affect a human form, something like my appearance now. Stephens died that night, after telling our story. Something like madness took him. After many more nights I felt my strength fade and I became imprisoned in this house, unable to step outside. As the years went by I slipped into dormancy, a still subsistence in which I saw much but was unable to act. I heard tales of a scarlet figure haunting the streets and I knew my wife had risen again.'

'You're here now,' said Richard. 'You've risen. How, after all this time?'

Daniel shook his head slowly.

'Something awoke me, prompted me to gather my strength into a semblance of humanity. I felt that something had changed, something in the ether. Elizabeth felt it too, and her restless spirit is drawn to us.' His face hardened. 'The time is near, Richard. We have work to do. It is time to destroy the Milbury Witch.'

The Witching Hours

* * *

Lucy's first instinct was to run, but her feet felt anchored to the floor, and she could merely stumble back a heel at a time. The figure in the doorway made no move to enter the house, but Lucy could feel it reaching for her nevertheless, in some abstract sense. She felt its influence rather than its touch and she fought it inside. She knew these apparitions were leftovers, fragments of years gone by that had clung on through time – although they might see her and attack her in those ways that they could, they had no true power here. She'd escaped the broomstick creature and she'd overcome her fear of the ghastly funeral party. This witch likely couldn't even cross the threshold. And yet... The power of the thing was stronger than anything else Lucy had felt tonight. It seemed more real too. The wake ghosts she'd seen that evening had been blurry and the stick creature had vanished after a few terrifying moments, but the witch was clear as day: a pale form draped in a deep red burial gown, raven-black hair veiling a pallid face. It stood poised but unmoving.

Lucy remembered the tale from earlier; the words of the man at the bar – *"They say she walks the streets of Milbury still, a woman in red, seeking those nearest the threshold of death... always she is grasping and clutching at those paths back to the living world"* – and guessed why the witch seemed so real. It was of the present, of Lucy's own time. It was no phantom of the past but a ghost of the now, a haunted creature wandering the village, seeking those nearest death. Lucy wondered whether it was her own untimely demise the witch was pursuing, and felt a deep and momentarily overwhelming sense of sadness and disappointment: she did not want to die yet: there was so much in her life she still had to enjoy. She loved her life. She didn't want it to end.

The witch raised its head, and its rain-sodden gorgon tresses fell back to reveal its face. *No*, thought Lucy: her *face*. For it was a beautiful face that even the kiss of death had been unable to damage. High cheekbones and full lips, a heart–shaped chiaroscuro of sepulchral shadows and bone-white flesh. Those eyes were arresting, deep and dark, and Lucy stared into them and felt a pull, a force that reeled her forwards. There was sadness in her eyes too, a pleading quality that plucked at Lucy's heart.

Let me in, a voice whispered, though the witch's lips did not move. *Please, Lucy. Let me in.*

Lucy stepped forward. The door swung a little as the wind and rain thrashed outside. *It must be cold out there,* she thought. *Someone could catch their death out in the storm.* She took another hesitant step. Those dark eyes begged her, implored her.

Please Lucy. Invite me in. I must come inside.

Lucy's mouth was dry as she parted her lips to whisper. The witch nodded slowly, encouraging her. Lucy was close enough to the door now that stray flecks of rain would alight on her face and chill the skin they landed on. The tiny studs of cold made her flinch just as niggling sounds cause a sleeper to fidget before waking.

Lucy woke from the witch's spell and cursed herself for falling under it. She shook her head at the red figure, refusing her in the most primal sign language, and turned her gaze from the witch's eyes. It was her right to refuse the ghost its entry and she felt a burst of triumph, a sense of victory at defeating the will of her supernatural tormentor. What confused her most was the witch's response – her pale face twisted not from anger, or frustration, but from pain and rejection. Those lips, once surely a red kiss, now a pale blue cry, mouthed at Lucy, desperate to reach through to her. It was as if her words could not cross the threshold. Was this part of her trickery? A ruse to gain access to the house, and to the vulnerable victim within? Lucy didn't know. She knew that she was thinking for herself now, knew the witch had ceased using magic to beguile her. Those dark, pleading eyes. Long white hands clasped together now, those lips pursed into a familiar shape:

Please.

Lucy held open the swinging door. A glimmer of hope passed over the woman's face. There was no malice in there – no hint of pleasure at a quarry all but cornered. Lucy was hesitant, but she was convinced.

'Elizabeth,' she said, out loud, over the batter of the storm. Those dark eyes never left her own. 'Come inside.'

And for a moment there was stillness, and to Lucy it seemed like the wind had stopped and the rain had ceased to fall. Outside, the woman closed her eyes, and for a second there was peace. Lucy's very heart seemed to have stopped. Then a rush, as a world fell back into place: the hammer of rain and bellow of wind. A flash of lightning – and the woman was gone. Lucy gasped. There was a roar behind her and she spun around to see the fire burning full and bright in the hearth. Sconces on the walls burst into flame, illuminating tapestries and furnishings. The heavy oak door was wrenched out of her hand and slammed shut, rocking the very foundations of the house. Lucy screamed then, in shock and terror. She wanted to run but had nowhere to run to – there was a storm all around her now, a storm of unnatural and strange power, and she was trapped within it. The whole ground floor – a Georgian entrance hall, parlour and lounge – was ruddy with the flames, and suddenly warm. Lucy spun, at once terrified and enraptured by it. As she turned back to the lounge she stopped dead. The witch was stood in front of her.

'No...' Lucy whimpered and stumbled backwards, never daring to take her eyes from the figure, ignoring the pain as she collided with columns and benches. The witch followed her till Lucy could retreat no further and held her hands up: a gesture of innocence.

'Lucy,' she said. Her voice was soft, a young woman's voice. Lucy had expected a rasp or a croak. 'Don't be afraid. Please – don't fear me.'

Lucy shook her head as if to dispel the apparition.

'You're the Milbury witch. Of course I fear you!' Her hands grasped against the plain wall behind her, clutching for some stability in the face of supernatural danger. The witch stepped away, hands still raised.

'I mean you no harm, Lucy. Please – I wish only to thank you for inviting me in. It took courage, and compassion. You did not believe that I meant to hurt you when you permitted me to enter.'

'That was before...' Lucy's head spun and her eyes darted about the room, taking in the complete transformation from present day public house to eighteenth century manor. Her heart still raced from earth-shattering slam of the door and the sudden explosions of flame from every torch in sight. 'Before you did this. Before you came in.'

'I did not intend to scare you! It has been over two hundred years since I last set foot in my house. It is of no surprise that the magic follows and surrounds me – reconfigures this place to align with my own memories of it.' Those dark eyes examined Lucy's face, taut with fear. 'I am not the demon I am reputed to be.'

Lucy realised she'd been holding her breath. Part of her – a large part – had expected the witch to kill her as soon as she'd invited her in. She wondered why she'd done it in the first place.

'Why are you here then? If you don't want to kill me.'

'I don't want to kill anyone.' The witch had moved closer to Lucy again, as if attracted by a magnet. 'I think I have some purpose to fulfil here tonight. I was drawn here this evening – drawn to you, Lucy. But something else has stirred too. Other forces are at work.'

'Yes! I've seen them for myself.' Lucy felt emotions that had bottled up inside of her threaten to spill out. Fear, confusion, curiosity... She bit back tears. The witch looked fascinated.

'What have you seen?' she asked. 'Ghosts?'

Lucy nodded. The witch's interest seemed inappropriate to her, but it was somehow comforting. It was a human emotion, and it invited trust.

'Something horrible. Like a scarecrow made of broomsticks. It chased me.'

The witch frowned.

'How remarkable. It must have been some shadow of a creature, its appearance warped by time and magic.'

'There was a funeral party too. Here, in the parlour.' Lucy realised her brushes with phantoms this night must seem underwhelming to a real ghost.

'The funeral...' The pale face frowned. 'Where I first met Daniel.'

A connection flared in Lucy's memory.

'Daniel. Your husband Daniel – he killed you. He hanged you! For witchcraft. For dealing with the devil...' Her voice trailed away. She was talking to something that had died; died many years ago.

'Not for dealing with the devil,' replied the witch. Her voice was laced with hurt. 'Though Daniel knew of that well enough.'

Lucy believed the witch: believed Elizabeth. If she'd wanted to kill her – or drain her life, or use her to regain her own existence – she could have done it already. She'd stopped her own powers and let Lucy invite her in of her own free will. She was trying to convince Lucy that she was no threat.

'You said you were drawn to me,' she said to the ghost. 'Why?'

'You have something of mine,' smiled Elizabeth. 'It's hanging around your neck right now.'

Lucy's hand shot to her breast and to the incarnadine teardrop hanging there.

'This was yours...' She felt guilty for wearing it when its original owner was stood in front of her.

'It still is,' Elizabeth murmured. 'I never gave it away, or sold it. I died wearing it, but woke without it.

No, don't take it off.' Lucy had reached for the clasp on her neck. 'It is yours now. I cannot take it. Its presence brought me here; brought me to you. I felt it as soon as it passed into the village. But it belongs to you now.'

'Then I'm the reason these ghosts have awoken,' said Lucy. 'I brought it here, and it summoned you, and the others.'

'No, Lucy. It drew me to you, but I have wandered the village for centuries, unable to rest. I entered a pact with my own husband, though when I did I knew not how deep his ambition ran, nor that a darker part of him was kept buried inside. He cannot rest and so nor can I. Our fates are tied. Only with his passing will I be permitted to die.'

Lucy remembered the story from earlier.

'Then Daniel is a ghost too? Where is he?'

'He haunts his house – this house. I have never been able to enter, for a mortal must invite our kind over the threshold. You are the first to see more than an echo of me since my death.'

Lucy thumbed the pendant around her neck, feeling the silver, warm under her skin. It reminded her of Richard.

'Elizabeth,' she fought down a rising dread. 'My own husband – Richard – I lost him this evening. I think he's slipped away. Is he in danger?' Her voice faltered as the witch's face grew grave.

'He is in the house? You're sure?'

'I don't know. I don't think he would leave in the middle of the night. He wouldn't leave me.' Lucy felt the prick of hot tears as she thought of her husband. 'What could have happened to him? Can the ghosts hurt him?'

Elizabeth's eyes were full of sympathy.

'The ghosts that you've seen tonight are but shades of the things that happened here. They cannot touch you or harm you. I fear only that Daniel's spirit may have found him first. The longer he stays with Richard, the more he will feed from his living spirit. Daniel knows something has happened tonight, he knows that magic is at work in this house. He is gathering his strength in preparation for my arrival – leeching from your husband to give him the power to fight me.'

Lucy's heart stopped. She felt numb.

'Can we save him?'

Elizabeth reached a hand forward, but stopped: a gesture of compassion prohibited by death. The sadness in her face hardened to determination.

'Come with me, Lucy.' The torches and fire brightened for a beat and the witch turned and walked to the staircase. Lucy followed uncertainly. The door at the foot of the stairs creaked open of its own accord and Elizabeth swept through, gown cascading up the stairs like a ruby waterfall. Where Elizabeth passed, the house changed and became as it once had been: a Georgian manor. Walls paled to a whitewashed hue and electric lights crackled into burning sconces. The witch beckoned Lucy from the top of the stairs and passed through a door to the left that Lucy was certain had not existed till now. Elizabeth's guidance was like the coming of spring to a cold and damaging winter; Lucy felt scared but assured, safe behind the light-bringing power of the Milbury Witch. As she passed through the new door, she felt a pang of hopeful longing and thought of Richard. For a moment she'd felt so close to him, as if he had been behind her all along, hiding, just a game. Lucy felt sad. The witch was striding through another door ahead of her. Lucy followed her only hope of seeing Richard again.

* * *

Daniel's head jerked round. Richard heard it too – a fumbling, wooden sound, like rats in an attic. It came from behind the wall. Richard made to ask what it was, but the words caught in his throat – he felt as if he were at altitude, in a place with thin oxygen. He coughed and spluttered out the words.

'What's that sound?'

Daniel scowled at the wall and stood up.

'Some witchery...' he muttered. 'She is here.'

'In the house?'

The ghost nodded.

'Not on this plane. She inhabits a darker realm, her own branch of existence.'

Richard took him at his word.

'Will she fight you? Can she hurt you?'

Daniel turned back to him. In the moonlight his skin took on a green-blue tint.

'Not if we hurt her first. Come with me.'

Richard hauled himself up and followed in the wake of the ghost.

* * *

Elizabeth led Lucy into a small room, little more than a cupboard. Lucy noticed there were no windows but she could see well enough – the witch lit the place with her very presence like a lamp in a dark sea. The room was scattered with arcane miscellanea, but Lucy's eyes were drawn to set of small straw figures – dolls made from twists of corn and twig. Elizabeth looked around.

'They seem familiar to you?'

Lucy nodded and picked up a figure with brush-like hands and feet.

'It chased me.'

'It wasn't real. There is a focusing of magic in this house tonight – it animates me just as it shone a lantern against the shapes of the past; against the silhouettes of my family at the funeral party. It may warp certain images, distort them and change their purpose. This doll was an innocent token, a charm against filth and disorder. It is earth magic; white magic. Its fellows are for health, prosperity and safety.'

Lucy replaced the doll.

'How do you know this? About magic and time?'

Elizabeth began to cut stems and grasses, dropping the ingredients into a cauldron.

'With death comes understanding. Certainly, I may have chosen different paths in life, knowing now what I do in death.' She took the straw doll from the shelf. 'This is the figure that chased you?' Lucy nodded and Elizabeth added it to the cauldron, before selecting bottles from the high shelves.

'You are a witch, then,' said Lucy. Elizabeth paused, white hand on a glass phial.

'In life, I was entrusted with certain knowledge,' she said, quietly. 'I knew how to prepare plants and herbs to ease sickness and ailments. I knew how to weave trinkets that eased the toils of everyday life. In time, I learned how to guide the weather – to hide the sun behind cloud or hasten the coming of a thirst-quenching rain. My witchcraft was of no danger, no threat to anyone. It came from the earth, not from heaven or hell. It never imposed, only assisted with motions that were already in place. It was not evil.'

Lucy thought about Richard and hoped that Elizabeth's craft could rescue him. She focused on the heart they shared – the love she felt for him, and of how deeply she knew he cared for her.

'Daniel branded you a witch,' she whispered. 'Your own husband. How could he?'

Elizabeth emptied a spherical bottle into the cauldron. There was no fire beneath it but the contents steamed as if heated.

'Daniel was not always a terrible man,' she said. 'But sometimes men are led astray. By things that cannot be helped.'

It caused her pain to discuss this, Lucy realised. She knew Daniel had murdered his wife in a brutal fashion – knew that he didn't deserve Elizabeth's sympathy. She let the witch continue in her own time. Elizabeth composed herself.

'Our attraction was instant, and reciprocal. Daniel required comfort on the night of his father's funeral, and I gave it to him. My family – those you met earlier in the parlour – left following the service, but I remained with him. It was what we both wanted. Publicly, we kept to our own chambers, on opposite wings of the house.' Elizabeth gestured around her. 'Of course, our true intentions were not quite so virtuous.' A hint of a smile shone in her eyes, some fond memory from long ago, soon to fade. 'The villagers talked, of course, but neither of us was disliked. I may have been a stranger but Daniel was a respected gentleman, and I was only ever kind to those around me. There was no malice towards us – not at that point. That I never swelled with child somewhat dampened rumours of our affair.'

Elizabeth ground a bunch of herbs in a pestle and mortar and added them to the pot.

'We wed after a year or so. My ways were unspoken but not unknown. I saw no reason to keep my craft a secret, not in my own home, not when I did what I could do to ensure strong harvests and prosperous trade. But Daniel became increasingly distraught at our failure to conceive – it gnawed at him. I found him more than once casting through my few books and journals as if the answer to our fruitless communion lay within. He came to blame me for this affliction, and placed the fault with me and my ways. He began to take occasional trips with trusted accomplices, staying away for weeks at a time and returning with things under his cloak, hiding away in his own chamber, nearest my own. In the beginning, I believe he wanted to cure me of my infertility, but as he explored the deeper channels of the craft, so his ambition grew, and his greed.'

The cauldron had begun to smoke, a rich resin aroma that filled the chamber. At first it tightened Lucy's throat and made her want to cough, but the sensation passed, and she let the potion fill her lungs and mind.

'I tried to turn him back onto the path of the right and good, but he pushed me further and further away. By the end, I think Daniel saw me as a threat. To kill me would have been the act of ultimate domination, of power.

For isn't power what all men lust after? His resentment grew and he wished for me to encumber his actions no longer. He came for me in the night as I gathered herbs beneath the full moon. I did what I could to escape but it was no good. He forced the rope around my neck and...' her voice faded.

'It hurt, Lucy. It hurt more than anything else in the world.'

Lucy reached for her hand. It felt cold but it felt real. Lucy's eyes stung from the potion smoke, and objects in the room pulsed in and out of focus. She felt as if the cell around them was the whole of the universe; that it was just she and Elizabeth left in the entire world. She wanted to comfort Elizabeth, though she knew the white witch was now a ghost, and likely beyond the touch of mortal sympathy.

But maybe I'm a ghost too, now, thought Lucy. She felt outside of herself. The cauldron simmered in front of her and Lucy bent towards it, into the dense and intoxicating spiral of smoke. Inside, a pool of khaki liquid seethed, stems and sticks breaking the surface like the masts of wrecked ships. The corn dolly Elizabeth had drowned in there bobbed up in the centre. It had begun to fall apart, its limbs frayed and water-damaged. Lucy peered at it. It was growing larger, rising from the depths like a surfacing corpse. Its face – *had there been a face before?* wondered Lucy – swelled and she stared into its woody eyes, the face morphing around them into someone she recognised. The cauldron was the door to another plane, a channel out of this tiny universe, and Lucy saw what she most wanted to see in the whole world.

Richard's face looked apprehensive, scared even.

His mouth was moving but Lucy couldn't hear what he was saying, and his eyes never settled on her own. She saw him as if through a filter: a pattern of wood grain and corn ears etched a tattoo into his skin as if a light was casting an odd shadow. *It's the magic,* she thought. *The magic is confused between Richard and the corn dolly.* She could hear odd words coming from the cauldron and she bent closer. Richard was speaking, but not to her. There were gaps in his speech as if she were hearing one side of a conversation. She strained her ears.

'Find her...' Richard's voice whispered. *'How to... we ...destroy...'* Lucy frowned at the words. Richard's face was troubled. *'Daniel... Daniel...'*

Lucy became aware of a cold and numbing sensation behind her, like the vague register of cold water running over already-frozen skin. She pulled away from the cauldron, her tiny world moving in slow motion, and came to kneeling on the floor of the chamber. Though she didn't remember blacking out, there was a haziness in her head that reminded her of a time she'd once fainted.

Elizabeth was knelt before her. Lucy guessed she'd been the one to pull her away from the face in the cauldron.

'Why did you stop me?' she asked. 'I saw Richard.'

'You were too close. Too much of the potion would have damaged your senses, dulled your wits.' Elizabeth's form flickered. 'I'm sorry, Lucy. You saw Richard. Where is he?'

'I don't know. He was talking to someone. I think it was Daniel.'

Elizabeth nodded.

'He found your husband first. It is as I feared.'

'They were trying to find someone.' The memories were already fading, dreamlike. 'And destroy them.'

'They mean to destroy me.'

'But why? I don't understand.' Lucy's head throbbed. The room felt stuffy and stale. She stood, a little unstable on her feet.

'Daniel attempted to kill me on that night two hundred and fifty years ago,' said Elizabeth. 'Perhaps there was more to his actions than simple jealousy. Something more that, left incomplete, has bound both his spirit and mine to walk this earth till Judgement Day.'

'He was carrying your body away from here,' said Lucy. She fumbled for the story she'd been told earlier that night, probing through the pulses of discomfort racking her head. Elizabeth noticed her frown of pain and guided her out of the smoke-wreathed chamber and into the fresh air of the hall, leading Lucy back towards her bedroom.

'Go on,' the witch said, and Lucy realised that Elizabeth did not know about the events following her own death.

'He hanged you,' started Lucy. 'Daniel hanged you and he ran away. The villagers called him a murderer and buried you. Your grave –' part of Lucy wondered whether it was untactful to mention this to a dead woman '– your grave is in the grounds of the church with the crooked spire. But Daniel came back. He dug you up and took you away. Took your body away, I mean. He was riding away from the village with another man when he was attacked by a thief and killed. The other man returned to the village and told everyone that you were a witch: that Daniel had dug you up in order to stop you rising from the dead.' Lucy stopped. Small pearly tears slid down Elizabeth's face.

'Go on,' the ghost whispered.

'That's all I know. I'm so sorry.'

'Don't be. What's done is done.' Elizabeth gazed out of the window, her glassy eyes settling on the grasping branches of that fateful tree. Her face was thoughtful. 'He needed me for something.'

'Needed your body?' Lucy cursed her bluntness of words, but there seemed to be no way of tackling these topics sensitively. Elizabeth didn't seem to take offence.

'Perhaps. There are many ways to tempt the attentions of the dark powers. Where was he taking my body?'

'I don't know.' Lucy thought hard – what had the man at the bar said? 'East...' she hazarded. She'd imagined the coach travelling the same road that she and Richard had driven in on. Had that been in her imagination?

Elizabeth thought hard for a moment before shaking herself out of her concentration. 'Forgive me, Lucy. There is no time to consider Daniel's purpose now. We must find your husband before Daniel does him damage beyond repair.'

'But where are they? How can we find them?'

'If Daniel means to destroy me tonight, there can only be one place he means to do it.' Elizabeth turned back to the window. 'That very same place whereupon he killed me a quarter of a millennium ago.'

She looked down, and Lucy followed her gaze, to

the creaking, moonlit tree far below them.

* * *

The night was cold. Richard followed Daniel out of the house and into the grounds – he doubted whether the ghost could feel the chill of the darkness, or the whip and spray of rain as it hurtled from the sky. The grass was wet and muddy beneath Richard's feet. He knew where they were heading; it seemed to him that the world of ghosts and magic was built on rituals and symbols, and what could be more symbolic than the very tree from which the sorceress Elizabeth had swung by the neck?

Whether or not this was the present, Richard didn't know. He felt that the fresh air outside was doing him well and guessed that, at the very least, this place was closer to his own time than the far reaches of the ghost realms to which Daniel had taken him that night.

They stopped at the foot of the tree.

'We're close, Richard,' said Daniel. 'The witch will come for us soon and when she does, we will be ready.' He stepped over the reaching roots of the tree and disappeared for a moment behind its trunk. Richard shuffled for warmth in the cold and wet. There was no cover from any other foliage; the tree was stood on its own, as if its destiny had been dictated at its very planting. There was a ripping sound, as if Daniel were tearing at the bark of the tree, and Richard edged after his guide. Daniel emerged, pulling a long box behind him. A coffin. One end of it dragged through the churned up grass, the other was held in the pale hooks of the ghost's fingers. He set it down on the flat grass beneath a protruding branch.

Richard thought he knew which branch.

'Do you remember what I told you?' asked Daniel. 'My plan was to bind the witch's spirit to her body and imprison her in a place from which there was no escape. I was stopped before I could succeed. Tonight, we complete the task.' He opened the coffin. It was not the romantic casket of classic horror but a plain rectangular box, unlined, unembellished. Inside rolled five grey nails, each around nine inches long, and a wooden mallet.

'I don't think I can nail her into a coffin.' Richard shivered. The thought of crucifying something, even an evil witch, filled his stomach with a whirlpool of ice. Daniel shook his head reassuringly.

'Nor will you be required to do so. Elizabeth has no earthly form; she cannot be restrained in such a fashion. Your charge is of a more metaphoric nature.' He gestured to the coffin and its contents. 'Take the nails, and the hammer. Pierce the casket as I instruct.'

Richard knelt in the muddy ground, feeling the brown water soak through his jeans and into his cold flesh. He grabbed the nails in one fist. They stung his skin as if he had seized a handful of nettle stems, and he dropped them onto the lawn. He picked up the mallet in his right hand.

'Place the first two nails here,' said Daniel. He motioned to the middle of the opened coffin: a silver stake for each side, as if to stab through each hand. The cold took away the bite of the nails and Richard drove them into the pale wood with soft but firm taps. Daniel scrutinised his work.

'The next two here.'

Richard shifted to the base of the box and

knocked in the pair of nails. The silver was a little malleable and the blunt heads flattened slightly under the hammer blows.

'Thank you, my friend.' Daniel's face was set in that victorious expression which Richard had noticed earlier. 'You are performing your task perfectly. These objects are of the mortal world, upon which I cannot act. You carry out this service with courage. I am indebted to you.'

Richard stared at the last nail, then up at Daniel. The ghost pointed with a long, spectral finger.

'Here.'

Richard edged on his knees to the head of the coffin. The nail prickled at his hand as he positioned it.

'A little lower,' instructed the ghost. 'Remember where it must penetrate.'

Richard arranged the final nail and raised the mallet. As it fell he had a sudden and unwelcome image; a silver stake stabbing down and into the witch's open mouth, cutting through the back of her throat and biting into the stained wood beneath. He swallowed his gorge and dropped the hammer. The nail trailed a long shadow in the moonlight.

'Excellent, Richard.' Daniel gestured Richard to rise and he did so, soaked from the knees down. 'You have done what I could not. All that remains is to seal the witch's spirit within.' He produced a length of rope from amongst the roots of the tree. It was old, frayed and stained. Nimble white fingers knotted the rope, five coils forming above the foreboding loop of a hangman's noose. Daniel swung the rope and left the noose dangling seven feet above the open coffin.

'The bait is placed and the cage is primed,' whispered Daniel.

'What now?' asked Richard. 'Will she come soon?'

'Very. All that remains is to wait.'

* * *

Elizabeth led Lucy through the ground floor of the house. As they passed, the Georgian lamps and tapestries melted away and the modern-day pub trickled back into view. The front door swung open ahead of them and Elizabeth stopped and turned to Lucy.

'You must wait here.'

'What? Why?'

'The events that are to transpire now will be fraught with danger.' Elizabeth frowned with compassion and sadness. 'I do not want you hurt – our time together has been fleeting but I hold it dear to me. You are back in your own time, on your own plane. You are safe here in this house.'

'But Richard is out there – he's my husband! I have to help him.'

'Not at the cost of your own life.'

'I don't care! I would let myself die if it meant he would live.'

'But would he want you to?' Elizabeth grew brighter, her form glowing red through her burial gown. 'If he would do the same then he would want you to stay here, safe. There is no sense in placing another life in harm's way. Please, Lucy. Stay here.'

Lucy was silent. She kneaded the pendant at her

breast, burdened with anxiety. Elizabeth's words made sense but Lucy's heart weighed heavy with helplessness and guilt. She must stay; Richard wouldn't want her to risk her life, and it was Richard she was trying to save.

'Elizabeth.' Lucy held the glass teardrop in her fingers. 'You said you were drawn to me because of this.' The necklace caught in the glow of the lamps and a ray of light glanced from its surface.

'Yes. What we possess in life may absorb some essence that we will always recognise, particularly those objects with great sentimental value.'

Lucy reached to the clasp on her neck and unclipped it. She pressed her lips to the red shard at the centre of the chain. It was warm. She held it out to Elizabeth.

'Richard bought it for me. It was his before he gave it to me – maybe he will be drawn to it like you were. Take it when you go to him.'

Elizabeth bit her lip, then reached for the pendant. For a moment it was caught between their hands, bridging the divide between the woman and the witch, the living and the dead. Lucy half-felt she could hear a hissing in the air, as if heat or electricity were thrumming between them. Elizabeth fastened the catch around her neck quickly, resting the chain and stone on the fabric of her gown.

'I will return it to you,' she said.

There was a pause, and Lucy imagined that Elizabeth was steeling herself for her task. Then the witch turned and passed through the doorway.

Lucy watched her for a moment before closing the door behind her. The iron knocker clunked softly on the other side. She felt at a loss – was she just to wait whilst the witch fought her battle? She wandered back into the entrance hall – now of course, the space between parlour and restaurant. Her gaze followed the line of the bar and settled on the conservatory. The moonlight was strong, the storm clouds finally thinning, and through the panes of glazing she could see the fatal tree. She moved through the house towards the conservatory, and caught a flash of red in the corner of her eye. Elizabeth. The white witch glided over the grey lawn towards the tree where, Lucy could see now, there waited two figures. One she did not recognise, but could identify nonetheless. The other was unmistakeable, its form and posture as familiar to her as her own reflection. Richard's face was framed by the hanging shape of a hangman's noose.

* * *

Richard watched the red figure approach and let Daniel step ahead.

'Be on your guard,' the ghost whispered. 'The witch will lie, and use her magic to deceive. Do not believe her words.'

The witch drew closer, her face grey and hard in the moonlight. Her gown was blood-red and her eyes were dark. Daniel stepped forwards.

'Elizabeth,' he called out. 'You have found your way back to me.'

The witch stopped some ten paces from her husband. Richard was reminded of a standoff in a black-and-white film.

'Daniel. It has been two centuries; if only we could resolve this matter peacefully. Instead, your wickedness and greed have prevented any chance of passing from this world to the next without violence. At least, won't you spare Richard? He has no part in our conflict.'

'You speak of wickedness and greed,' parried Daniel, ignoring her request. 'Your pact with the devil has imprisoned you on this plane, cursed you to walk the cold night for eternity. My communion with you has led to my own incarceration here. I will end it tonight, with your true death.'

The weakness Richard had felt in the far reaches of the ghost world had returned and he felt drained and powerless. He remained still, trying to avoid the attentions of either spirit, and his stomach lurched as the witch turned to look upon him.

'Richard,' entreated Elizabeth. 'I've met Lucy. She led me to you. You must not believe this devil.'

'Lies,' hissed Daniel. The two ghosts had begun to circle one another, like cats ready to fight. 'You know what must be done. The witch must be laid to rest, once and for all.'

Richard's gaze passed from the combatants to the deadly coffin at his feet, the nails within glistening like the teeth of a bear trap. Elizabeth's eyes followed his own.

'Silver,' she breathed. 'You would imprison me in this casket? To what end?'

Daniel's face was a snarl. His form had begun to shimmer with a faint green light.

Richard turned back to the witch.

'You've seen Lucy? Is she safe?'

'Don't speak to her, Richard. Do not permit entrance to her spells.'

'Yes, Richard, I've seen Lucy.' The witch was drawing closer to Richard, closer to the tree. 'She's safe, but she will be in danger if Daniel is to defeat me here tonight. He has surely told you nothing but lies. He does not mean to lay me to rest at all.' She cast a fearful glance at the coffin before returning her attention to her husband's ghost. 'You were riding on the stone road, taking me towards the sunrise...'

The noose hanging from the ancient tree was swaying slightly. Richard had taken it to be caused by the wind and rain, but now he noticed a thin green luminescence surrounding the rope. It twitched, the hanging tip rising a little like the head of a serpent.

'Do not listen to her Richard,' Daniel warned. 'Can you see your Lucy? The witch has likely used her to gain entrance to my house and then killed her to serve her own needs.'

'No Richard, please.' Elizabeth begged as Daniel shook his head. The witch drew ever closer to the tree and the flicking rope hanging from its branch. 'It's Daniel who has lied to you; he has been draining your spirit this whole night. He slew me in a fit of jealous rage all those years ago and then...' her form blazed red for a moment. She hissed at her husband. 'You were driving towards the Henge, were you not? That well of ancient magic. What dark ritual would you have performed there? Is this why you have had this prepared?' She strode to the open jaws of the coffin. 'You monster. Your greed has no boundary – even in death you wish to violate my spirit and for what? Some taste of infernal power?'

Daniel advanced on the witch.

'No,' he growled, quietly. 'All the power. All the

powers that the sacrifice of a witch will grant me.' He raised his hand and the hanging rope darted, slipping around Elizabeth's neck. Her scream was cut before it could form and she was jerked up to hang, precious inches above the silver stakes below.

Richard was frozen. Daniel turned to him.

'You see, Richard.' The ghost's blue lips peeled upwards in a grin of triumph. 'We have won. The witch is apprehended. You did well to deny her lies.'

Richard mind was whirling. He watched the struggling witch twirl on the end of the emerald cord like a fish caught on a hook. The body twisted towards him and he saw the familiar flash of a red and grey chain against her breast.

'Lucy's...' he choked on the words. He felt dead on his feet. The world around him began to blur: only Daniel's form seemed clear to him now. 'Lucy's necklace...'

Daniel cast a languid eye up to the dying spirit.

'A trophy. She killed your wife and robbed her corpse just as her own body was plundered.'

Richard blinked hard. The world was fading to an indistinct haze, as if his own spirit was fading. As if from a long way off he heard the sound of breaking glass.

Daniel drew a long dagger from his coat; an ugly iron blade that seemed familiar to Richard. He stepped up onto the thick root of the tree and reached for the rope above his wife's neck. He smiled at her, a ghastly grin.

'This is the end, fair Elizabeth,' he murmured. He raised the knife.

'Richard! Richard!'

Daniel turned angrily and Richard raised his head.

A white figure was running towards him, a white figure bathed in moonlight that he recognised beyond a shadow of a doubt.

'Lucy...' he whispered.

Daniel stepped down from his perch and extended an arm wreathed in green fire, but Lucy sprinted past him and fell to the ground beside her husband. He felt heavy in her arms; a dead weight. She clutched his head to her body.

'Richard, Richard, wake up, please...' She held a hand to his chest but could feel no heartbeat. His breathing was shallow. 'He's drained you Richard, but you're alive, still alive. Please Richard, wake up...'

The ghost of Daniel advanced on them. Lucy gasped and crawled in front of Richard.

'You bastard. Leave him alone! Why did you have to do this to him? He's not yours to harm. He's mine.'

The ghost glowed with a strong green light and Lucy knew its power had been fed by her husband's spirit.

'She was mine before she failed me,' whispered Daniel, pointing his dagger at the still twitching Elizabeth. 'All things die. We do what we can to keep ourselves alive.' He lunged for Lucy and the ugly blade descended, a blow to the heart that seemed to dive in slow motion. Lucy screamed, eyes scrunched shut. The blinding pain never came. Lucy cracked her eyes open.

The knife hung an inch from her skin, blocked by a glow of red fire. She gasped and leapt back from the blade. Daniel's ghost was pushed backwards, landing in a heap on the ground. Lucy's head spun towards the witch on the rope. The pendant round her neck – *my pendant*, thought Lucy, *my pendant from my husband* – blazed like a star. And Lucy realised that this was not Elizabeth's doing but her own. She felt a piece of the white witch inside herself, a streak of Elizabeth's spirit that had been absorbed into her just as Daniel had absorbed the spirit of Richard. The fire around her was her own, an extension of her passion and fear, and she pushed it outwards – not at Daniel in anger but at Elizabeth. The green noose coiled round her neck stretched and snapped, and the witch fell to the ground beside the coffin. Lucy felt the magic inside her fade and she fell back to the ground, exhausted.

Daniel's ghost picked himself up and stalked towards Lucy. His face was ugly and twisted. The knife was clenched in his ghostly fist and he pointed it at her.

'She was mine to kill. Not yours to save.' His head whipped around. Elizabeth loomed behind him. A dark green welt burned around her neck.

'Fair husband,' she breathed, 'this is your end.'

The witch wrapped a hand behind Daniel's head and pulled him close to her. She kissed him on the lips, holding his face against her own with one hand, fumbling behind her neck with the other. Lucy saw a metallic glimmer in her fingertips – *silver,* she realised. As Elizabeth held her husband still, she twined the necklace around his throat and pulled.

There was a searing sound like meat hitting a hot pan. A strangled groan – Daniel, as the silver burned through his hollow throat. Elizabeth, too, grimaced in pain, and Lucy saw the silver must be scalding her hands as she grasped the chain tight. The two ghosts fought for a moment but Lucy could see battle was over. Elizabeth pulled the chain free, ripping through Daniel's neck and out the other side. She dropped it as if it were molten, and it fell to the ground without a mark.

Daniel's ghost swayed on its feet, flickering like a moon reflected in water. There were ragged holes torn through its throat and a sluggish translucent fluid oozed thinly from the torn white flesh. It fell backwards, its graceful glide now an unnatural oily stagger, towards the tree. The nails in the coffin glinted in the moonlight and the ghost was sucked down upon them as if drawn by a magnet. Lucy closed her eyes and wrenched her head away with a scream as the topmost nail stabbed cleanly through the dreadful twisted face. The lid swung shut and trapped the ghost inside.

There was stillness in the night.

Lucy held Richard close to her. She was more scared now than she had been facing any ghost or spirit this evening. Her husband was cold and pale, as still as death. She glanced around and saw Elizabeth sweeping towards her. The witch radiated a soft red warmth that seemed to enter her and banish the horrifying images of the last few moments. Her own fear, however, remained undiminished. The witch knelt beside them both.

'Are we safe?' asked Lucy. She glanced fearfully at the coffin.

'Yes. The silver affects our kind in a potent fashion. To be fixed like Daniel has been is to be fixed forever.' Elizabeth glanced down at her own hands, striped with deep red welts. 'Daniel will fade soon enough. The nails are poison and will destroy him in time. He will be forced to face his judgement on the other side.'

'What would he have done with you? Killed you?' Lucy stroked Richard's face. Elizabeth's face darkened.

'He would have taken me away from here, to the stone circle across the plain.'

'We've been there,' said Lucy.

'Such places are like folds in the fabric of space. Could you feel it? They are closest to the more abstract realms – portals, or channels, just as this house was tonight. Daniel had no doubt uncovered some black ceremony, some sacrificial ritual that used a witch's death to unlock great power. He would have...' Elizabeth cast her eyes down to Richard. 'He would have slain your husband and used his death to return to the mortal plane, after using him to ensnare me.' She gestured to Richard's hands, and Lucy saw they were burned and blistered. 'Daniel could never have prepared the cage without mortal assistance. But Richard had lingered too long in the ghost world – enough for the silver hurt him too.'

'Will he get better? Will he be ok?'

'I do not know.' Elizabeth reached out but stopped herself from touching him. 'It was his time away from his own world that sapped his life; Daniel simply stole his essence when he could. Care for him, and I should think he will recover.'

The witch reached for the pendant lying on the grass, picking it up by the glass shard. She proffered it to Lucy.

'I promised to return this to you.'

'I don't want it back.' The images had begun to fade, but Lucy knew the necklace had killed someone – even if that someone was already dead. She couldn't forget that.

'It has power, Lucy. It was a gift of love to you; I cannot think of anyone who deserves it more. Take it –

seal it in a box if you wish, never look upon it again. But keep it, own it. It will pass its power on to you.'

The chain hung from Elizabeth's hand. Lucy took it. It felt cold and damp from its spell on the ground.

'Thank you,' she said.

The night was slowly giving way. The moon was low in the sky and the stars had disappeared, but the world was lighter. The sun would rise soon.

'What will happen to you?' asked Lucy. She knew that Elizabeth and Daniel had been imprisoned together, that neither one could move on without the other. 'Are you... Are you still trapped here?'

The witch looked puzzled.

'I have laid my husband to rest; his evil has been thwarted. I wandered the plain for centuries before the opportunity to defeat him arose, knowing my task was to save others from his wicked design. And yet... I feel unfulfilled. There is something more that must be done.'

A quiet note of birdsong curved through the garden. The air felt clear after the storm, and a narrow ray of light sliced over the horizon.

Elizabeth's body began to glow, a deep orange-red, the colour of sunrises and sunsets and the eternal passing of years. As the halo intensified, Elizabeth's body began to fade, and Lucy watched as the radiance uncoiled and flowed into the body in her arms, entering above the heart. The witch smiled as her ghost slipped away into the light of the morning sun. Richard's eyelids flickered, and Lucy turned her face up to see Elizabeth, now little more than a faint shape hanging in the air.

'Thank you,' whispered Lucy, warm tears trickling down her cheeks. Elizabeth's lips moved in reply, but her words were silent. Lucy looked down into the eyes of her husband, and when she turned her face back to the sky, the witch was gone.

Lucy realised the rain had stopped.

* * *

The morning air felt clean, fresh and mild. They'd woken late to some pointedly loud vacuuming from out in the landing at checking-out time, and had had to forfeit their offer of breakfast. That was fine. They could stop somewhere on the way home.

Lucy took the driver's seat with Richard squeezing in behind the hatstand. For a while they drove without the radio but with the windows cracked open, listening to the steady rustle of the countryside around them. They passed a church with a crooked spire pointing up towards the heavens, and patches of forest where the sunlight fractured between twigs and leaves, shining out as if from a golden lantern. They passed through small villages and hamlets, where wooden signs and coats-of-arms proclaimed histories and idiosyncrasies. They passed the turn-off for a national heritage site; a prehistoric stone circle. Sometime around midday, they stopped in a picturesque little town for a bite to eat.

After a pot of tea for two and a sandwich apiece, they took a walk round the town, stretching their legs before the home run. Lucy spotted a deep red drawstring pouch in a gift shop and decided to buy it – it would suit her new necklace perfectly and keep it safe from harm. The sun was still shining when they returned to the car. Richard flicked the stereo on as Lucy drove, scanning the stations till he found one he liked, and that Lucy would too. They drove steadily – there was no rush to be home. It was a pleasant autumn day, and winter rains were miles away.

The Witching Hours

About the Author

Liam Smith enjoys writing quietly, drumming loudly and dressing in black. He hopes you enjoyed reading this book as much as he enjoyed writing it. If you feel like contacting Liam, visit his website at
www.liamsdesk.co.uk
or send him a message on twitter:
@HoraceCSmith
He would love to hear from you.

Printed in Great Britain
by Amazon.co.uk, Ltd.,
Marston Gate.